DRAGON'S FATED MATE

RED PLANET DRAGONS OF TAJSS BOOK 18

MIRANDA MARTIN

CONTENTS

1

CALAUN

The empty sands stretch out ahead, bleak and unending. Once I found them beautiful, but that was long ago, before the world lost its appeal.

Now there is only honor and duty.

A warm breeze tugs at my wings as I run across the sands. The suns are low on the horizon and it is clear I will not make it home tonight. I do not mind. They do not expect me for another day. My mission was a success. The Commander will be pleased. Our ability to monitor the territory is now greater than before with the placement of the signal repeater.

It should, ideally, restore communication with the Order's leaders. I had no idea that we had lost contact with them, but then why would I? That is definitely a need-to-know piece of information and I did not need to know.

This is the way of the Order. It is how we rise above our base instincts. How else would we resist the constant call of the bijass, that driving urge to return to our more primal states? Even now, its call is inviting. It would be easier to let go, to forget all that I am and live only in the moment.

While most of my memories are lost to the fog that the

bijass brings, I still recall too much. I remember the pain and the loss that the Devastation brought, even if the details of it are lost in the aching grief of the past.

My view to the horizon is blocked as I run down a dune. Temptation calls for me to run through the night. It is dangerous but life on Tajss is dangerous. What do I care for facing danger?

My Commander's voice echoes through my thoughts, reprimanding me for once more putting myself into danger. I smile as I recall the last time. One of the giant zemlja was burrowing its way towards the compound. These animals, like colossal worms but with a huge mouth lined with rows of teeth at the tip, are one of the most dangerous creatures on Tajss. Somehow our deterrents, so carefully placed around the Order's stronghold, had not held this one back.

Tracking picked it up, and when it became clear it was not going to turn away, the decision was made to fight it. That is never an easy decision. The zemlja are a manifestation of Tajss itself. They are the planet's lifeblood in so many ways, but the greater mission of the Order could not be put into danger.

I was chosen for the team to fight it, and when we engaged with it, the fight was as expected. Hard, almost impossible. The zemlja burrow through the ground, leaving the massive tunnels that offer shelter to over half the plants and animals on Tajss. They turn the sands causing more fertile land to rise to the surface, allowing the small crops we grow inside our compound. Some say that wherever the zemlja go, they spread life in their wake. And without them, there would be no epis.

Epis. The jewel of Tajss, the queen of plants. No one in the galaxy would have been interested in Tajss if not for epis. Epis grows only here in all the known universe, and it has so many properties that it became the most sought-after thing ever imagined.

Too sought after. So much so that it inevitably led to war, which in turn caused the Devastation. The Devastation that took everything from me.

The hints of a smile forming on my face die as I dodge the memory that tries to come along with my thoughts. It is not one I want to recall. I do not need to see the source of my pain yet again. It is always with me, waiting, hiding out of sight, still too raw to confront.

Instead I focus my thoughts on the fight with the zemlja. Tribyana had failed to dodge quick enough as the zemlja burst from the ground, capturing him in its mouth. He fought, but his legs were into the creature's throat, being swallowed, and he was barely holding himself out as it tried to digest him.

The rest of the team wrote him off. Unfortunate, but there is no saving someone in that state. Or there shouldn't have been, because it was so incredibly dangerous. His screams cut through me though, pulling at my buried memories. I couldn't stand it, so I acted.

I ran at the undulating body of the zemlja and dodged as it slammed the ground, trying to crush me. Tribyana's arm was broken in that slam, but I leaped and landed behind the thing's round body. Wings spread for balance, I ran up its body to its mouth and drove the point of my lochaber into it.

The creature screamed in pain, opening its mouth. As Tribyana slid further down its open throat, unconscious from the slam, I grabbed him and leaped to safety. The zemlja rose into the air and then dove for us. I did not stop running, carrying my fallen brother in my arms.

We barely escaped, but we did. My heroics were not crowned with laurels. I had been punished for a week after that for my disregard of discipline and obedience.

I shake my head to clear it of memories. My legs burn as I climb the next dune. I have been running since the suns first rose and I'm growing tired. It would never stop me, but it could slow me down if I do run into something that I'd have to fight.

Cresting the dune I stop, closing my outer lenses to filter the light, and stare ahead. Rolling dunes in shifting shades of red stretch to the horizon. The two red suns blaze fiercely as if they're fighting to stay above the rim of the planet. A warm breeze stirs the sands as it drifts over my scales.

Something screams.

Instinctively I pull my lochaber off my back, resting the shaft in the crook of my elbow, the blade pointed forwards. A low growl, then another scream. I don't see a source, but I sense the direction and run.

The growl comes again, louder. I'm at the bottom of the dune and climbing the next. Two screams echo this time, high-pitched and oddly… they sound human. There shouldn't be any humans out here, especially alone. All the humans are at the City or the caves with the Zmaj who call themselves the Tribe.

I'm far from either of those locations. None of our records indicate humans in this area. When the scream comes again, all doubts of the source are gone. That's a human sound. No creature on Tajss has that pitch.

"Siara run!" a female voice screams.

Female. Human. Here?

Doubling my speed, I spread my wings and leap to catch the warm drafts of air and glide ahead faster. The dunes in his area are massive, but the sound of their voices tells me I'm close. There are more screams and growls as I reach the crest of the dune. Then I see them.

Four human females have encountered a lone guster. Even one of those creatures is proving too much for them.

The females run, but one of them has one of the electro-sticks the humans have invented from materials left by the aliens they call the Invaders.

The guster's attention is on one of the runners, but the girl with the shock stick runs to it, not away, in an act of incredible bravery and stupidity mixed. She slams the shock stick against the guster's thick hide. It's not enough to damage the creature, but it certainly gets its attention.

The large head swings around blindingly fast, and sharp teeth snap at the female. She stumbles back, barely staying out of range, but her feet sink into the sand, and she falls over backwards landing on her rear.

She scrambles backwards, but the guster has her. It moves closer, sniffing the air, enjoying the scent of fear on what is about to be its meal. Unless I can stop it in time.

"HERE!" I yell, leaping into the air with everything I have.

Wings spread, tail waving, I glide through the air, my shadow passing over the fallen female and the guster, the twirling lochaber whistling. The female looks past the guster, eyes widening and mouth dropping open.

The guster moves, whipping towards me lightning fast, causing my strike to miss. The blade of my lochaber slices past its head, and I crash into it.

Foul breath assaults my senses as it snaps, trying to get a bite. I dodge, twisting to one side, wrapping my legs around its middle. It thrashes wild, desperate to dislodge me.

I tighten my legs, holding on, and struggle to get a grip on its head. It screeches, calling for help. Guster travel in packs, and I need to end this fast before more of them arrive.

Its leather skin is thick and slick, giving me no purchase. It twists and turns, bucking, and knocks me off. I punch it in the side of its head, and it yelps, then darts its head forward for another bite. I dodge its teeth, but it slams up, catching me under my jaw.

My head is snapped back by the force of the blow, causing stars to blind my vision as pain explodes in my head. The bijass swells from the deepest parts of my mind, lying claim to my thoughts. The female is under my protection. I cannot fail.

Blindly, wildly, I fight the creature, slamming it over and over with my fists, the lochaber dropped and forgotten. I'm aware of the cuts on my fists, because some of my punches have connected with its teeth, but I'm as frenzied as the guster.

It fights. So do I. We slam into each other over and over. It nips my arm, drawing blood, which angers me further. We both drop as one to the desert floor, and my leg is pinned by its weight. It goes still, so I lie on the warm sand, letting the red rage of the bijass pass.

When my thoughts are my own again, I place my free foot against the guster and fight my way out from under. The females have huddled together a few paces away, staring. The one I saw with the shock stick is in front, holding it up defensively.

"Stay back," she orders, speaking passing Zmaj.

I rise to my feet and brush sand off before giving my attention to them.

"Sure," I say, holding my hands up.

The lochaber is sticking up from the sand off to my left, but I carefully make no motion towards it. The female stares haughtily, looking down her nose at me. The three with her are frightened but doing their best to hide it.

I like this one. Something stirs in my thoughts, but I push them down. She's pretty, for a human. Blonde hair and a nice frame but more than her looks is the appeal of her dominance. She is a leader, obviously, and not going to be bossed around.

I like that, even if it's a bit frustrating at the moment.

"Who are you?" she asks.

"Calaun," I answer. "You?"

"Annabel," she says, defiant. "What do you want?"

"Want?" I ask, genuinely confused. Did I not just save them?

"Yes, what do you want?" she repeats.

"Well," I say, thinking this through. What do I want? "Are you hungry? We could harvest this meat."

"Yes!" two of the females behind her say in unison.

I step forward, but Annabel threatens me with the shock stick, so I take a step back holding my hands back up.

"We don't need your help," she says.

"Yes, we do," another of the females with her mutters.

The female spares a glancing glare behind her before returning her full attention to me. I could leave them, but what honor would I have then? Humans are woefully unprepared for life on Tajss, and they are females. They should be protected.

"Where are you from?" I ask, trying to get somewhere with this.

"Nowhere that matters to you," the lead female, Annabel, says.

"We're heading to the City," another of the females answers.

"Damn it RaiAnne, shut up," the Annabel snaps.

"Annabel, we need his help," RaiAnne says.

"At what price?" Annabel asks, glaring at me. "What do you want from us?"

"Want?" I ask, shaking my head. "I was on my own way. I do not want anything from you, but I don't want to leave defenseless females alone."

"We're not defenseless," she says, brandishing the stick.

"Of course," I say, deciding not to argue with her.

She's confident to the point of arrogance, but I like her.

I've only interacted with a couple of the human females, but they weren't like her at all. Confident, certain of herself, but behind the façade, I sense more. Pain. Pain that calls to me, pulls at my own memories.

"Let him help us, Annabel," RaiAnne says.

"I'm starving, let's eat," another of the females says.

"If we accept your help, you'll let us go?" Annabel asks, eyes narrowing.

"I could escort you to the City," I offer.

"Why?" Annabel asks.

"How about we harvest this meat before it spoils?" I ask, changing the question.

"Fine," Annabel says, lowering the stick at last.

Slowly I take the hunting knife off my side, and continuing to move slowly, I kneel next to the guster. My knife is well cared for and sharp, so it slides into the base of the guster's throat easily. I pull it down along the front between the bones of the breast plate. As the beast is opened up its guts spill out.

I grab the skin and make a slice along its shoulder and another along the haunch, then pull the skin back to reveal the succulent meat. One of the females gags as I work, but Annabel watches with cold interest.

The suns are below the horizon by the time I finish harvesting the meat. The females have remained huddled together watching and waiting, though I don't know for what. Annabel stays in front of them, and they occasionally talk among themselves. They speak in their own language when they do, which I don't comprehend.

Once I've harvested the meat, laying the cut pieces out on the drying skin, I set about creating a small fire. I take a few pieces of wood from my pack and scrounge the area for some dried brush from rolling weeds to use as tinder.

Kneeling next to the carefully arranged wood, I place my

face close enough that my flames will reach. Then I belch a burst of fire. The kindling catches and in moments a small fire is burning. Once it's established itself, I lay out the pieces of meat. Some I thread onto a stick that is placed to hang the meat in the flames, and the rest I lay out on small stones around the fire to slowly cook and smoke for preservation.

"Oh man that smells amazing!" one of the girls says. She speaks Zmaj too, though with a strong human accent. I must speak simply to these females.

"We'll have food shortly," I say. "May I know your names?"

The females all look to Annabel before any of them answer. Annabel glares, then shrugs.

"I'm RaiAnne," the dark-haired one says, but I'd caught her name earlier. I nod and smile in what I hope is an encouraging way

"I'm Siara," another of the females says. This one has red hair that is almost the shade of the sands.

"I'm Ella," another says. She has brown hair and a pinched nose.

"I'm Nina," the last one says. She has light-brown hair and her nose is her most prominent feature. She has a resigned air about her.

"I'm Calaun," I say, repeating my name. "I'm happy to help."

"Still don't need it," Annabel mutters.

"Yes, we do," Siara snaps. All of these females speak my language well enough to argue in it.

"This piece should be good to eat," I say, getting a piece of the cooking meat out.

I toss it hand-to-hand to cool before handing it to Siara who takes it with a big smile and immediately sets about devouring it. Annabel glowers, watching the other woman eat, but I can't take my eyes off her.

Stirrings, deep inside my soul, shift. An old calling so long buried I barely recognize the changes. I want her.

It's a pulsing sensation that aches. Demanding satisfaction, pushing the fog of the bijass forward with its primal nature. The small fire casts an orange glow, outlining her perfection. The other females fade in my vision as she dominates the world around her.

Her jaw tightens, eyes narrow, and a thin sheen of moisture forms on her forehead. Her head is tilted back so she would be looking down her nose at me, if not for the fact I'm a head and chest taller. Her lips part, and as they do, the slightest of tremors quakes them. The pulse in her throat is rapid. Her breath is shallow, and the more I focus it's as if I can hear her heart racing.

She's afraid. Afraid to lose control. She hides it behind her façade of anger and dominance, but there is not a doubt in my mind. It calls to me, echoing through my thoughts and tugging at the suppressed memories. Memories of loss and pain that even now I don't dare recall.

Overriding the shifting sensation comes a roar. A fire that races through my limbs, burning away all in its path.

Treasure.

She is my treasure. The dragon has chosen.

2

ANNABEL

He won't quit staring at me. As we sit and eat the food he prepared, his eyes are on me constantly. Every time I glance over, he's watching. It's annoying. What the hell is wrong with him? Look at the others why don't you?

The ring on the finger of my right hand is heavy. So heavy it's hard to lift the meat to my mouth. Quintin, I miss you so much.

No, I'm not going to feel sorry for myself. This is my life, here and I'm going to do what he would have wanted. I'll make the best of it, but that doesn't mean I'm going to forget either. None of the girls appreciate his sacrifice as I do. They don't really appreciate how much I do for them.

They'd all be lost without me, but do they appreciate it? No, they don't. Chewing on the tough piece of meat, I study them as I try to keep my mind off the strange Zmaj who won't quit staring.

They're okay. In another life I might have liked them, but there's no point in getting close to anyone here. As soon as you do, they'll be gone. Lost or running off with a dragon mate of their own. Or out-voting me and deciding we should all move to the City.

I don't want to move to the City. I don't like Rosalind, for one. She's dominating and has to be in control. She's an arrogant bitch, and I don't need anyone telling me what to do. Besides, what do we need from the City? Gomul has given us all the help we'd ever need, but no, these girls can't appreciate a good thing when they have it.

The back of my neck itches, so I look over and there he is, still staring. His eyes are heavy, seductive if I was looking for that, but I'm not. I'm not against the alien-human mating per se. I'm against any mating and me though. I had my mate and he's gone. That part of me is over. I'm a different woman now than I was then.

"We should pack the rest of this meat up," I order, standing up.

Full dark has fallen, and we didn't make as much progress as I would have liked. Now we have this guy to deal with, and I wish he would at least stop staring!

"Give me a minute," Ella says.

"A minute for what?" I snap. "You doing something so all-fired important that you can't help us preserve this food for later?"

Ella's face colors even in the light of the fire as I rebuke her.

"Take it easy, Annabel," Siara says.

"Why?" I ask, whirling on her. "Why should I? You think I'm not pulling my weight around here? Are you?"

I don't want to be yelling at them, but it's automatic. Instinctive. Yet I'm sitting here in my own head, watching myself be a total bitch to the girls. It's stupid, I should just stop, but I can't. The words keep pouring out of my mouth.

"Annabel," Siara says, rising to her feet, hands on her hips. "That's enough."

"Enough what, Siara? You think we're going to make it out of this if we're not careful with our supplies?"

"I'll pack it up," Ella says.

The strange Zmaj watches passively, not speaking or moving, but continuing to stare at me, and that pisses me off even more.

"Don't worry about it, Ella," I bark . "Obviously I'm not pulling my weight, according to Siara, let me do this for you, too!"

"Annabel, I didn't say that," Siara says.

"You don't have to spell it out for me," I say. "I'm not stupid. I know what you mean."

Siara throws her hands up in frustration as she snaps her mouth shut. Ella is trying to pack the meat, but I push past her and do the work. I slam meat onto the dried pieces of oiled leather, wrap them up roughly, and tie the strings to keep the wrapping shut. The first piece of string won't tie, and my frustration builds, tears welling in my eyes until I can barely see.

Hands touch mine and I jerk back, looking up. It's him. Damn it. I wipe at my eyes furiously, drying them on my sleeve, and glare.

"I've got it," I say, jerking the package towards myself.

"Of course you do," he says, and he's not being sarcastic. There isn't a hint of rancor in his voice or his demeanor. He means it.

What in the hell is wrong with him? When I look into his eyes, my heart beats faster. That primal instinct built into my core throbs, but I shut that down fast. I don't care how big, muscular, and sexy he is. Those damn Zmaj, running around with their twelve-pack abs hanging out because they refuse to wear shirts. I'm not going to scratch that itch. I'll never be disloyal to Quintin. No matter what.

A small voice whispers through my thoughts that he'd

want me to move on, want me to be happy, but I squash that too. I don't deserve to be happy when he doesn't have the chance. He died trying to provide for us. The rest of them may be willing to forget that and move on, but I'm not.

Defiantly I tie off the package of meat and throw it to Siara, who adds it to our packs. The Zmaj packs up a piece himself as I grab the next and do my work. The anger drains away. I wish I had a better handle on my emotions. On the ship they'd probably have put me on some kind of meds. Something to take the edge off, keep me calm. There are no meds here to take, and I'm left dealing with this overwhelm of emotions.

And a stupid Zmaj who can't leave well enough alone. Let's not forget that.

Emptiness aches in my core, so I do what I always do when it hurts. I twist his ring on my finger and bite my inner lip, letting the best memories of our life play through my thoughts. It hurts, every single time, but by the time I'm done I do feel calmer.

"We should sleep," I say. "Nina, can you take first watch… please?"

"Sure," Nina says.

"I can watch," Calaun offers.

"How many times do I have to tell you we're fine?" I ask. "You can go… do whatever you do. We'll be fine."

He smiles and shakes his head.

"Yes, you will be," he says. "But I'd like to help. Please."

I glare in an attempt to burn the smile off his face but to no avail. Finally I shrug and shake my head.

"Fine, do what you want," I say.

I find my blanket on the small sled of supplies we'd packed before leaving Gomul and heading for the City. After picking a spot at the edge of the small fire's light, I spread out my blanket, then lie down on one end of it and roll it around myself. I lie on my side with my back to the fire, not wanting to see Calaun—or any of them for that matter.

As I lie there on the soft sand, my arm for a pillow, my thoughts drift to where they always go. The love of my life. Or so I thought. Quintin.

He'd been perfect. Kind, brave, willing to put up with my shit. He was smart too. A scientist on the ship, working on top secret projects. The one thing he wasn't, though, was a warrior. Still, he was a man, and he did what men do. Tried to be manly.

Except that wasn't my Quintin. The man I loved was a nerd. A gangly, skinny nerd who was never cut out to be a provider on this hellhole of a planet. Losing him still hurts. It doesn't matter how long it's been, it's not long enough.

I drift towards sleep, remembering making love to him for what would turn out to be the last time. As my mind shuts off, the man panting on top of me shifts from Quintin to Calaun, and with that, I fall asleep groaning in pleasure.

I wake up stiff, sore, with one hand between my legs applying just enough pressure to be pleasurable. For a moment I lie there enjoying the erotic sensations, and then I wake up enough to realize what I'm doing and where I am.

I sit up with a start.

The Zmaj sits a few strides away, still staring. The suns haven't crested the horizons yet, but the sky is lightening. Cheeks flushing hot, I sit up quick, looking to get my bearings. No one else is awake yet, leaving me in the awkward position of meeting gazes with Calaun.

"Good morning," he says softly.

"Good morning," I say, unable to continue the eye contact.

Did he see? Did he know what I was doing while I slept? My face is so hot. It feels like it must be written across it that I was dreaming of him in a very sexual way. Shame fills me as snippets of the dream come back to me. Quintin would never approve of this.

I need something to focus on besides the memories, so I climb out of my blankets. I carefully fold and roll them, then replace them on the supply sled. The fire has died down to nothing more than a pile of ash, which is fine. I'm not hungry, and I don't want to ask the Zmaj to restart it.

"We should get going," I say, moving to Siara and kneeling.

"You could let them sleep," Calaun says. "They're exhausted."

"I could, but then we'd end up walking through the hottest part of the day and taking even longer to get to the City. How about you let me run my show, and you do… whatever it is you think you're doing."

He holds his hands up in surrender with that same infuriating smile on his face. Half of me wants to wipe that smile off. It looks too much like a smirk. As if the smile itself is saying he knows better than I do.

I'm being stupid. I know it, and I wish to hell I could stop it, but here we go again. I'm on the emotional roller-coaster that I've been riding since Quintin died. It's been so long. I think it might be years now, but it still feels as fresh as if it happened yesterday.

Maybe it would help if we could keep track of time, but we've been a little too busy for that. Survival isn't easy here and hasn't left much time for idle pursuits like building calendars or clocks.

"Wake up," I say, shaking Siara gently.

She groans, rolls over, then sits up bleary eyed.

"Good morning," she says.

"Morning," I respond as I move to Ella.

In short order, I have all the girls up and putting away their packs. We're used to running on only one meal a day, and since we've been doing it so long, no one is hungry yet. Having no need to eat anything, we set off on our course. Ella takes her turn pulling the sled first.

Calaun falls in beside me as I lead the way. He doesn't say anything and only rarely do I catch him watching me out of the corner of my eye, but I'm acutely aware of him. He dominates the space with his presence. We travel in silence, and I'm grateful for it.

There's an awkward conversation to be had here, but if he's not going to bring it up, I'm not either. We march slowly, making progress until the suns are directly overhead beating down on us. This is the worst part of the day. Gomul advised us not to travel during it, so we stop and use our blankets to make a rough shelter to hide from the suns.

"This is very clever," Calaun says, examining our makeshift tent.

"Thanks, I was really hoping you'd like it," I say, feeling snarky.

Ella and RaiAnne both snort, but Calaun seems to miss the sarcasm.

"I'll keep a watch while you rest," he says.

"You didn't sleep last night," I say. "If you're going to insist on being our chaperone, then you need to be sharp."

"No, I didn't," he says. "But I'm well trained for this."

"No one can be that well trained," I snap. "So how about you do what I say and don't be an ass?"

He tilts his head with confusion written across his face.

"What is an 'ass'?" he asks.

Only then do I realize I'd slipped a Common word into the sentence.

"You, if you don't listen to me," I say rather than answer as my cheeks warm.

"Nice," Siara says.

I give her a glare to shut her up. It's all I can do to keep a lid on the storm roiling inside. Losing face in front of the few remaining members of my group pushes my buttons and makes me want to lash out. Which is stupid, I know it, but then there we are.

"Can we rest now? You, Calaun, take a rest. I'll stand first watch."

He stares, unblinking, and I meet his gaze unflinching. Slowly a smile spreads over his lips and he nods. "As you wish."

Siara and Ella exchange a fast look, mouthing *'Princess Bride?'*

I don't know and I don't care. That's the line and I'm going to hold to it. No one on the planet has vid-sticks, so there's no damn way he could have seen the vid. If he did, then there's a whole hell of a lot more going on in the City than we know about.

Calaun, for his part, ignores the looks. He walks over to beside the tent and lies down on the sand. He lies on his side, his tail stretching up his back, over the top of his wings to curl over his shoulder. The girls stare, watching him instead of getting their rest.

"Sleep, now!" I bark, waving the shock-stick in the air.

They shake their heads then enter the tent and lie down themselves. I get a waterskin from the sled and take a small, conservative sip. I replace it then lean against the sled, letting it hold my weight.

The suns are straight overhead, beating down mercilessly. Sweat pours down my forehead, stinging as it reaches my eyes. I should chew some epis, but I'll put it off a while longer. I hate it. The damn plant is addictive, and we all know it. It's a hopeless situation though. What else can we do?

Humans aren't meant to live on Tajss. Maybe if we had a fancy dome and nice buildings to live in then we wouldn't need it, but all those jerks in the City are taking epis too. I've avoided stimulants like this my entire life. Even on the ship I didn't drink or do any recreational drugs. I can't stand not being in control of myself. When everyone else was experimenting, I spent my days trying to understand why they thought being out of control was 'fun' and not a nightmare scenario.

My worst dreams are ones of not being in control. Like when Quintin was… no I'm not thinking about that. The sweat stings my eyes worse and I'm forced to wipe away the tears. They're tears of pain, salty sweat hurts in the eyes. That's all they are.

The Zmaj twitches, jerking my attention to his prone form. His wings rustle and his tail is vibrating. Is he… dreaming? If that's a dream, then I'm guessing it's a nightmare. Good dreams don't make you tense up like that. Well, not if you're a human. I don't know that Zmaj even dream, much less have nightmares.

I'm fascinated by him. Okay, I'll admit it. I kind of like having him around. It's almost as if a little less of the weight is on my shoulders. It'd be nice to have someone I could lean on instead of being the one responsible for keeping everyone alive.

The hairs on the back of my neck rise. Rubbing it I try to shake the feeling something is wrong while I'm still contemplating the Zmaj but it grows worse. It's as if I'm being watched…

Instinctively I throw myself forward. I'm partly sunk into the sand which trips me, and I face-plant, breath rushing out in a whoof. Sand burns in my mouth and eyes. A harsh shriek cuts through any sand in my ears. Cold chills race down my spine as a shadow flies over me.

When I roll onto my back to see what's going on, a large pterodactyl-looking thing is climbing back into the air, having clearly missed its dive at me. I open my mouth to scream, but rough sand clogs my throat, and all I manage to do is cough.

Another shadow falls across and then Calaun glides over. I roll to one side, covering my head with my arms. There's a thud. Then something wet splatters across my back. I keep scrambling forward, fighting the loose sand for traction.

Finally I manage a yelp then a strangled scream to alert the others that we're in danger. I'm almost to the tent when two large claw-toed feet land in front of me. I look up, but I'm blinded by the double suns. I blink rapidly and Calaun is there, outlined in a glowing halo by the backing of the suns. He reaches down, offering a hand, but not touching me without invitation.

"What's hap—"

"Oh—"

"Annabel!"

The other girls emerge from the tent, and my cheeks burn hot as I take Calaun's offered hand. I'm a fool. A damn fool at that. I let myself drift into a stupid, self-absorbed daydream, and it almost cost us everything. Or me everything.

As much as I hate to admit it, Calaun saved my life. Again. Damn it. Now I really do owe him. Something anyway. Respect, yes. That's plenty. I'll try to treat him a little nicer.

"I'm fine," I say, turning to face the girls. They're pale and shaken.

"Uh, are you sure?" Ella asks.

"Yes," I snap. "I wouldn't say I was if I wasn't."

"You don't look so fine," Siara says, and the other girls nod in agreement.

Only then do I look down at myself and realize I'm covered in blood and bits of god-help-me. My stomach lurches, betraying my cool exterior, and it's all I can do to keep it down. One hand over my mouth, I glare at the girls, daring them to say a word. Silent, I walk over to the sled and dig for clean clothes.

"I'll harvest this meat, too," Calaun offers.

"Thanks," I say. I don't miss the looks the three girls exchange. "What?"

They look at each other as if daring each other to speak up.

"Are you *sure* you're okay?" RaiAnne asks.

Frowning, I stare her down and then nod sharply. "Yes."

Ignoring their stares and muttering, I dig through the small pack of clothes. My hand touches a cool piece of metal. I recognize it instantly, and the empty ache in my heart throbs. It's Quintin's watch. The one piece I've kept, my sole connection to him.

It's broken, and keeping it is stupid, but I can't bring myself to get rid of it. It's all I have left. He loved this watch. He said it was handed down to him through generations and helped him to stay anchored. Funny, now it's the anchor holding me to him. It keeps his memory alive.

Pushing it further down in the pack without looking at it, I grab one of my three shirts and then pull out my one other pair of pants. Welcome to life on Tajss. Nothing extra and everything is about survival. I turn on my heel, march into the tent, and pull the flaps closed behind me so I can change.

A small voice says to change here. Let him see me, give him a full view of what he's been staring at. That voice is stupid, so I tell it to shut up.

3

CALAUN

The painful ache that lies beneath the fog of the bijass lying across my past has become a constant. Every time I look at her it throbs with a life of its own.

Logically, I should stop looking. Why keep doing something that makes you hurt? Logic isn't playing a part in it though. I can't stop watching her. It's not her beauty alone that enraptures my attention. It's something much more than that.

She's been hurt, and that is what holds my thoughts. I want to find the thing that hurt her and destroy it. Obliterate anything that would dare to harm her. That drive is primal, instinctive, from deep in the nature of a Zmaj. It's not who or what I am now. That doesn't mean it's weak or that it's easy to ignore.

Escorting these females to the City is off mission. I should be returning to the compound, reporting in, and seeing if the new transmitter fixes our communication problem. I should be helping with the work of the Order. There is so much to do—our duty is unending. Serving Tajss is my highest purpose, especially now that she is under attack again.

The humans call them Invaders. It's an apt name, if not accurate. They are invaders, but they're a race those high in the Order know are called Pertinaxians. We fought them before, in the war that resulted in the Devastation. One of the many races that vied for control of Tajss.

Their return bodes ill for the planet. I should be working to stop their interest in the planet. An interest renewed after all these years shortly after the humans arrival. None of us are fools, it's clearly not a coincidence. There is some tie between the human ship crashing here and the return of the other races.

The humans don't know any of this. The Order has not yet decided to share these truths, and it is not my decision to make. I am not of sufficient rank to be involved in such decisions.

I focus on the carcass in front of me, and the harvesting of meat. The creature clawed down my chest before I killed it to save her. Blood is dripping from the wounds where two of its talons cut through my protective scales. Once I'm finished, I'll need to tend to the wounds.

Annabel emerges from the tent. I sense her approach like the soft drifting of a warming breeze. The other females approach with her, but I don't stop my work. This needs to be done now, and it's easier not to look at her. The ache, gone but not forgotten, is easier if I don't look.

"Let me help," Annabel says from over my shoulder.

"Of course," I say.

Best to let her have her way. Her tongue is as sharp as her temper. I'm not looking for a fight with her, though I can't say I don't admire her fiery temper. In a lot of ways I think I understand it. That pain she feels, how else do you deal with it?

Anytime I'm too close to my own lost memories I get the same way. Knowing that only serves to strengthen the feeling that she and I are connected. That on some level we belong together. If I followed the old ways, the ways before I joined the Order, I would accept it as fate. A primal choosing where my dragon knows its mate on sight.

Why I deny that, I'm not sure. It's not spoken of in the Order. We follow the Eye and his visions but there is nothing in those that says we should turn our backs on the old ways. There haven't been any females for it to be considered, though. Not in too long to recall.

Annabel moves to the far side and kneels, then stops, looking at my chest.

"You're hurt," she says.

"It is nothing," I say.

"Don't be an idiot," she says, rising and moving to stand in front of me. "Come on."

"The meat should be harvested first," I say.

"The girls will handle it," she snaps. "Now, come on."

I look at the other females, and they do move in, setting to work on finishing harvesting the meat with obviously practiced hands. When I don't move fast enough, Annabel puts her hands on my shoulder and pushes, forcing my attention back to her.

"Now," she demands, nodding her head towards the tent behind us.

I follow her towards the tent. She ducks inside, pulls out a small stool, and sets it on the sand. She manhandles me, pushing and pulling me until I sit on it. My weight pushes it deep into the loose sand, but it finds purchase before I'm all the way down.

She turns to the sled and digs through the packs there before turning around with rags and a small clay jar in hand. She opens the jar and I recognize the scent of the healing salve. She dips her fingers into the jar and layers the salve over the first of my wounds.

My hearts leap into hyperactivity as my mind empties of all thoughts but her. Her touch is surprisingly soft and gentle. She layers the salve over the first wound, then leans close to the second, inspecting it.

"You've got dirt in it," she mutters, shaking her head.

She turns back to the sled and retrieves a water skin. Holding the mouth of the skin at the top of the wound, she pours a trickle of water down the wound. I shiver at the cold.

"Don't be a baby," she whispers, intently watching the wound.

She dabs at it with a rag, biting her lip as she works. I clench my jaw, ignoring the pain of the rag in my open flesh. Once she's satisfied it's clean, she covers the wound with salve, then straightens to inspect her work.

"Bandages," she says, returning to the sled again. She pulls out a shirt and holds it up looking at it then at my chest. She shrugs and shakes her head. "It will have to do."

She grips the cloth between both hands and then tears it into strips. She ties the strips around my chest covering the wounds. Once finished she steps back to admire her work. A small smile tugs at the corner of her lips but she suppresses it.

"Better?" she asks.

"Very much so," I say. "Thank you."

She waves her hand dismissively, but I snatch her hand and hold it in my own. My hearts pound hard, making me feel the pulse in my neck. Our eyes lock onto each other, and for a moment, everything around us stills as if the world itself is holding its breath.

A flush creeps up her neck onto her cheeks. It's the color of the setting suns, soft reds. She pulls her hand from mine, but slowly. She averts her eyes from mine and swallows hard.

"It's... nothing," she says. "We should... quit wasting time. Let's get a move on. If we're going to get to the City, we should do it."

She glances at me surreptitiously, and I don't miss the looks, but I'm not going to push her. In my core the dragon roars, staking a claim that my rational mind isn't sure I want or need. The empty ache throbs worse as the dragon makes its will known. I'm left torn, uncertain in a way I've never felt before.

Nodding in agreement with Annabel, I rise to my feet and pick up the stool. I help the females to pack their sled and then we're traveling again. This time I decide to bring up the rear. I need the time to think through what is happening as I try to sort out my feelings.

The soft touch of her hands left its mark not only on my scales but deeper. So much deeper. The sensation dances through my thoughts. I can't shake it, but every time it comes to the forefront that sense of emptiness throbs, pushing the joy of her touch away. Rejecting it.

The females are strong, each independent and headstrong, but none of them compare to her. *Treasure.* The dragon whispers, invading my thoughts, pushing its desire. They talk softly among themselves, but Annabel holds herself apart.

My observations about the group make it clear she's the leader. She holds herself apart, not really above, but separate. A leader is the one who must make the hard choices. This is known in the Order. Those with rank don't fraternize with the lower ranked. Your decisions can well mean the death of those you lead. That weight is impossible to carry if you are their friend as well. A leader needs that objectivity and distance.

The sense of loneliness she exudes is the mark of a leader. My arms ache to hold her. I want to bring her comfort from the burden she bears. The hunch of her shoulders as she walks, the way she glances back at the others though they never notice. The longing on her face when she does. The edge of despair as she walks, holding it together against the impossible odds.

Five females surviving the desert. Alone? They must have had help. The shock-stick was designed by the City and that is their goal but how did these five females end up out here? So far from the City or the Tribe?

Two of the females slow their pace until they are walking on either side of me. Our pace is slow to begin with. The humans don't travel well on Tajss, but they try to not make it obvious what they're doing. It is, but I see the effort they put into it, so I play along.

"Hello," I say.

"So," the one they called Siara says. "How is it you came across us just in time?"

I can tell that she's only trying to open dialogue. If she was actually digging for answers, that would be a problem. My mission and the capabilities of the Order are not to be made known.

"Hunting," I answer. "It was luck that I happened across you when I did."

"Luck," Ella says. "I don't really believe in luck. Do you Siara?"

"Luck...," she trails off then shakes her head. "Nope. Fate maybe? Perhaps you were meant to find us?"

"I would not presume to know the will of fate," I say but my eyes are on Annabel.

My hearts race, my prime cock stiffens, and the rumble in my core disagrees. Fate. Yes, the dragon says, yes it was.

"Oh, he's wise too," Ella laughs.

The sound of her laughter makes me want to hear Annabel laugh. How could I bring her such joy that she would? Siara lays a hand on my bicep and I look down frowning, distracted from my thoughts of Annabel. When I glare at her she jerks it back.

"Sorry," she mutters.

"It is fine," I say.

I didn't mean to scare her, but the air between us has changed. She looks past me to Ella and shakes her head ever so slightly.

"Well, we appreciate it," Ella says. "A *lot.*"

She emphasizes the last word. I'm not sure why, so I look at her trying to read her body language and understand what she means.

"We wanted to *show* our appreciation," Siara says, so I look at her.

They both have their lips pursed in such a way that they look pouty, too full. They're leaning slightly in, and then it hits me.

"Oh," I say in surprise, the syllable slipping out before I can stop it. "Thank you, but appreciation is not necessary. A male protects. It is the way."

"The Way," Siara says, sounding the simple word with a reverence that makes it sound like a religion of its own.

Heat radiates off of them like the sands. They're close, too close. They barely take their eyes off of me and now I suspect there is more here than I would first have thought. I open my mouth to correct her but stop myself. Let her believe what she wants, especially if it will extricate me from this situation. Annabel glances back glowering, and her look serves to confirm my suspicion.

I'm not interested in these females, though now, I can assume they are interested in me. My brethren at the compound have spoken in hushed whispers about how the humans act. How different they are from our memories of

Zmaj females. I hadn't put credence in those rumors. It seems I was wrong.

A Zmaj mates for life. The joining of male and female is as sacred as the lifeblood of Tajss itself. Like the zemlja burrowing through the sands a male and a female's joining brings life in its wake. It is not something we undertake lightly.

I could be wrong too. What do I know of humans and their customs? What I do know is that Annabel is glaring unhappy, and that holds my attention. I'm the source of pain for her in some way, and I must fix it.

"Excuse me," I say. Lengthening my stride, I leave the two females behind and move to Annabel's side.

"What do you want?" Annabel snaps.

I contemplate my answer before giving it. What do I want? Pain throbs in my chest and deep in my thoughts.

"To help," I answer.

She snorts, shakes her head, and glances over her shoulder.

"Looks like you're doing a fine job of that," she says, staring straight ahead.

Frowning, I glance back too, trying to understand her thoughts. Siara and Ella walk close to one another, whispering. When they see my glance they smile in response. I nod in acknowledgment, but it's clear to me I'm out of my depths. There are currents here that I can't comprehend.

"Have I done something wrong?" I ask.

Her gaze snaps to me, eyes burning with a fire that calls to the dragon in my soul, igniting its flaming breath. That fiery breath blasts, burning its way through the very fabric of my being. I stop moving, left breathless in its wake.

"Wrong?" she asks, stopping too, her voice raising. "What could *you* have possibly done wrong? I didn't ask you here. I don't need you. You're not mine to order around, so what could you have done wrong?"

Confusion swirls in my brain, and the bijass reacts with its roiling fog urging me towards primal instincts. That primal part of my brain wants to grab her, kiss her, show her I'm a dominant male and worthy of her strength. Demonstrate to her that she can put down her guard, because I am here to protect her. Her anger isn't anger, it's fire, and I see that clearly.

She lashes out from past pain. Anger is her shield, the rock on which she has built her strength. Anger keeps the hurt at bay. If I sweep her off her feet, wrap her in my arms, hold her tight to my chest and push my lips to her, then she would know. She is safe. I will never let anything hurt her again.

That primal urge hits fast and hard, and I take a step closer before I stop myself. That is not the way to handle this. Except I don't know what to do. She stares, waiting, and I should say something. Do something but nothing comes. The raging of the dragon is loud in my ears, like the galloping thunder of a herd of stampeding bivo. Dominating my thoughts, urging me to stake my claim. Show her I am the one.

"Well?" she asks, hands on her hips, lips trembling.

Small drops of moisture form in the corners of her eyes. Her lips tremble, the color of her cheeks turns pale, and still she waits. Defiant. Expectant. Dominant and absolutely the most beautiful creature or thing I've ever seen in my life.

"You're beautiful," I say, my voice soft.

Her eyes widen, her lips part, and she takes a step back. There is an instant, the briefest of flashes, where I see her. The real her, not the façade she puts forth as her shield against the world. Her—real, vulnerable, wanting a mate who is worthy of her own strength.

It's a momentary insight that is gone as soon as it happens. Her mouth snaps shut, her eyes narrow, and she shakes her head.

"Idiot," she mutters, turns on her heel and resumes marching. "Someone switch with RaiAnne, she's pulled the sled long enough."

I look after her as she marches away until I realize that the other four females are staring from a huddle around the stopped sled. My scales itch and I'm uncomfortable, so I nod then walk over.

"I could pull the sled," I offer.

"Thank you," RaiAnne says, slipping out of the harness they've rigged for it.

I slip the leads over my shoulders and pull, walking fast to take the lead. Head down, I let my thoughts roam free and do my best to ignore their stares.

4

ANNABEL

Damn it. Damn him. Damn this planet. Damn these women. Damn anything and everything.

My thoughts circle while I do my absolute best to quit staring at him. As if there's anything else on this god-forsaken place to look at. Empty sands, rolling dunes, and most of the time nothing more than the red striated ridge we're climbing.

And he looks damn good.

He pulls the heavy sled easily, as if it's nothing. Jerk. That thing is heavy, loaded with all our worldly goods. Our lives are on that sled, defined by the few meager belongings and the necessary items for survival. Food, water, carefully wrapped epis. He walks as if it's nothing. All our stuff, nothing. Which only serves to remind me that that's all it is. It's nothing but a handful of stuff we've cobbled together from the wreckage of the life that was and the one we've fought to build here.

And, of course, he looks good.

Damn it, I need to get my thoughts under control. What

in the hell am I thinking? Sure, he looks good. Got it, great, and? Am I going to act on it in some way?

The ache in my chest throbbing at the thought tells me the answer as if I didn't already know it. I can't. The ring on my finger is suddenly heavier, pulling my arm down and making tears well in my eyes. When will they stop? It's been so long, but every damn time it still hurts so much.

"Are you okay?" Nina asks, appearing beside me and causing me to jump.

"Yes," I snap, blinking away the welling tears before they can form.

"Uh-huh," she says, staring.

"What?" I ask, shaking my head.

"It's okay," she says, keeping her voice soft despite my shitty attitude.

"What is?" I ask, getting my wild emotions under control.

"To hurt," she says. "But more importantly, to feel."

She pointedly glances at the Zmaj when she says this. I follow her gaze to him too. It's not only that he looks good. No, that's easy enough to ignore. He's been nothing but kind and helpful, and my outbursts don't phase him in the slightest. Quintin would want me to move on. I know he would, I'm not stupid.

If only I knew how to. Every time I get close to letting go, I'm jerked back. It's me. I know it's me, but I don't know how to fix it.

"Sure," I say, hoping she'll go away.

I know she means well, but I don't have any answers, and her help is only making the pain worse. She doesn't, though, instead she moves closer and puts an arm around my shoulders, pulling me into a hug. I stiffen but bear my way through it.

"If you need a friend," she says, her eyes boring into me. "I'm here."

"Uh, thank you," I say, staring straight ahead to avoid the sympathy in her eyes.

She nods and falls silent but stays at my side as we continue our journey. It's easy to fall into an almost trance-like state when you're traveling on Tajss. One foot forward, fight the rear foot out of the loose sand, take the next step. It's lulling, which is also why it's dangerous. Lack of awareness will get you killed. It's not the only thing that will, but it's a factor.

I don't want sympathy. We've all been through hard times. I'm not special, and the only answer to the pain is to push past it. Work harder, do more, make a difference. Besides, when they look at me like that, it make the ache worse. It forces me to think about how I'm not really in control. None of us are. Any of us could be gone in an instant. The same way he is.

Quintin wasn't a warrior by any means. He was a software engineer, a far cry from the type of man who would survive here. He was a nerd, super-geek even. Loved his anime, which I never could understand, but when he'd talk about it, he was so passionate that it made me interested.

Still couldn't watch it though. It was in some old language I didn't speak, and I sure as hell wasn't going to learn it for the "pleasure" of watching a vid. My eyes sting with goddam tears for the millionth time, and I don't want to wipe them away because then she'll know I'm crying. Again. So I blink furiously before they roll down my face.

Nina grabs my shoulder, jerking me to a stop. I look up to snap at her, then my throat clenches shut as I hear the low rumble. The sand dances and we all turn in circles trying to spot the direction of its source.

"Run!" Calaun yells, motioning.

Jerked from my internal misery I glance back and make sure the other girls are moving before taking off myself.

Calaun moves to one side and continues motioning us forward.

"Where are we going to go?" I ask.

"There is a crevasse over the next dune," he says pointing. "If we get there, they might not see us."

It's a glimmer of hope and not much of one. The rumbling is growing louder. It's definitely mechanical in nature but the only ones who have machines aren't friendly. Zzlo or the newer Invaders, neither of them will have good intentions towards us.

Nina trips and I stop to pull her up.

"Go!" she yells, eyes wide with terror.

"Not without you," I say, pulling her to her feet.

We run side by side, but I'm watching the others over my shoulder.

"Hurry," Calaun says, staring at the horizon. "We're too slow."

"What do you think they're doing?" I ask, heart pounding in my throat. His tail twitches, quick motions from side to side, then he leaps towards the slower women. "Wha—"

I cut the word off before finishing as he lands between Siara and RaiAnne. He grabs them both around their waists in a single motion, then spreads his wings and runs. He's fast. I had no idea anyone could move so fast on the loose sand of Tajss. In what seems an instant, he's carrying them past me.

"Hurry!" he yells, passing me by.

I don't wait any longer either, running with nowhere near the grace and ease he does. With every step, I sink into the loose sand, which slows me down. I fall behind but not too far. The rumbling is growing louder though, as fear crawls along my spine, making my knees weak. A stitch forms in my side, but I push on.

I still don't see what's coming when I look over my shoulder, but it sure is coming. Zzlo? Invaders? Some new threat?

Why does this place suck so much? As I look ahead, Calaun drops out of sight along with Siara and RaiAnne.

My foot sinks in extra deep as I find a particularly soft spot in the sand, and I jerk forward. I pinwheel my arms and stop myself from face-planting, but it takes precious moments to free myself so I can take the next step. A shadow falls over me as I struggle, then I'm lifted into the air.

"Ah!" I cry out in surprise, instinct screaming to fight, but before I struggle I am able to push down the panic. Calaun has me. A sense of relief rushes over me. For an instant I feel something I haven't felt since before losing Quintin. Safe. Protected.

I wrap my arms around his neck and let him carry me. The sensation relaxes tension in muscles I didn't know were there. He leaps and warm air rushes past, the warmth welcome against the cold chills of terror.

We arc down, and my stomach drops too. I suppress a new yelp before it slips out, then we land in a puff of sand. He sets me down next to the other girls, but his hands linger on my hips, his eyes on mine. His lips part and a desperate desire to taste them flashes through my brain. It can't be more than an instant, but time stops as this singular moment carries forward.

Then his mouth snaps shut as he looks up. The loud rumble is closer, too close. He crouches and leaps into the air. The suns outline him as he crests out of the shadow. His wings spread, muscles rippling as he pulls the long, shafted weapon off his back, pulling it around to ready. He's a shadow against the backdrop of the bright light, but it's magnificent. I tremble in awe as my mouth dries. I can't take my eyes off him until he disappears from sight.

"Shit, shit, shit," Ella sobs, dropping onto her ass and pulling her knees up to her chest.

Her cursing breaks the moment. Duty calls, she needs me.

They all do, whether they want to admit it or not. That's not fair, they're not ungrateful bitches like Kate was. All I've done has been to protect these girls.

I drop down next to Ella and pull her against my chest, stroking her hair and making soothing sounds. She grasps me with the tightness of desperation. I get it. This place is terrifying, and this is a straw too far.

The other girls kneel around us adding their arms and all of us huddle giving what comfort we can as we wait to see what's going to happen. If Calaun hadn't come with us this would be an entirely different story. We'd never have made it to even this much safety.

We wait as the rumbling grows louder and louder. Waiting with bated breath, racing hearts, and the inevitable sweat pouring off of us. Then the rumbling stops. None of us breathe. No one moves. Waiting. Hoping.

Hope is dashed with the sound of steel on steel. He's fighting. Alone against god only knows how many. Our fates rest in his hands. My heart pounds as anger rises devouring the fear. I'm not some fairy-tale princess waiting for a man to save me. I'm not going to some dark fate without a fight.

I squeeze Ella tighter, then move to stand. The girls cling to me, but I break free of them as I rise. They look up from their huddled positions, fear written across their faces.

"I'm scared too," I whisper. "I'm terrified, but I'm not going to let him fight alone. We have to be smart, but I don't care how good he is, one Zmaj alone against how many? One or two, he'll probably be okay, but what if there are more? We can't wait here to see if he saves us or not," I say.

They're so scared they're trembling. I don't blame them, I am too. My hands shake as chills race up and down my spine, but it doesn't change my mind. I'm not going to wait here to be captured or killed. If I'm going down, then I'm going down fighting.

"Right," Siara says, her teeth chattering but she stands.

The other girls follow her lead as I take the shock stick off my side. The sounds of battle continue hidden from sight. Closing my eyes I take a deep breath, tightening my grip on the handle, then I nod.

"Okay," I say. "We have to be smart. I'm going to sneak that way." I nod to my right. "I'll try to peek over the edge and see what's happening. We can't run into this blindly."

The girls nod, silent, none of us wanting to attract attention before we're ready. I press myself against the rocky, sand-covered wall of the crevasse and make my way along it. The top edges down the further along I go until I'm crouching to not be seen above it.

The girls are watching. I force a smile that I don't feel in the slightest, feigning an air of confidence I don't have. They're clutching each other waiting. It's time to find out what's happening. Good or bad.

Slowly I rise up until my eyes crest the edge of the dune. My heart leaps into my throat, and I drop down the moment I do. Pressing my back to the wall, I swallow hard, trying to force my heart back to where it belongs. This is bad. Really bad.

There are six Invaders. Their blue skin and four arms distinctly identify them as not Zzlo. As if Zzlo would be any better. Calaun is holding them off, but there are six of them. How do I help?

The Invaders are massive, the same size, if not a bit bigger, than the Zmaj warrior who's single-handedly facing them all down. The problem is one against six. Those aren't bad odds, they're impossible. Sooner or later, he'll make a misstep. One mistake by one man is the balance our lives hang in. We have to help. Somehow.

Staying low, I make my way to the girls. I contemplate our options to help, which are limited. We've only got one shock-stick, and going hand-to-hand with an Invader isn't an option.

"There are six Invaders," I say. They gasp softly but no one breaks the silence further, waiting for me to have a bright idea.

I wish I had one. The sounds of the battle continue, then someone screams in pain, and I can only pray that it's not Calaun. As soon as I realize that, pain stabs into my chest that is much more than concern for us. Concern I can't allow myself to feel. Instantly I see Quintin being torn apart and bile rises in my throat.

"We have to help," RaiAnne says.

"Yes," I agree, pushing away the horrific memories. "The only thing we can do is try to distract some of them. Buy him time to take them out."

They girls nod understanding and agreement.

"How?" Nina asks, her voice cracking.

I bite my lip and grasp for a bright idea. "We become targets."

"What?" Siara gasps.

"Targets," I say. "There's nothing else we can do. We can't fight them. We have one shock stick," I wave the weapon. "And it's not well charged. It probably wouldn't last an entire fight if they weren't twice our size."

"How do we do this?" RaiAnne asks.

"You, Siara, and Ella slip down to that end of the ravine, then run. Run away, fast as you can. RaiAnne and I will go back that way and do the same. Once we're running, split up. Make as many targets as we can. Circle out wide, then come back towards here."

"This is insane," RaiAnne breathes. "Insane, but you're right, this is our best shot."

"Right," I agree. "Anyone else?"

No one speaks up, so we divide and head for our respective ends. When RaiAnne and I are crouched beneath the edge, I look back and see the others are in position. I nod, then leap into motion. RaiAnne runs away as I instructed her, but I don't.

I didn't tell them this part of my plan because they didn't need to know. It's my duty to protect them, no matter what it takes, and this is what it takes.

The six Invaders are in a semi-circle around Calaun. He's turning slowly to keep them all in sight. In his hands is the preferred weapon of the Zmaj, a lochaber. A long thick shaft with a curved blade mounted to one end. The opposite end of his is also sharpened and looks like it has steel or some other type of metal on it. He holds the sharp blade out with the pointed end sticking behind him.

The Invaders look past him to the running girls. The biggest of the Invaders barks something and motions with two of his arms, and three of the six of them break off their fight with Calaun to chase the girls.

Perfect.

One of those three spots me, and an evil smile spreads across his nasty face. He runs across the sand easier than I do, which pisses me off. Is everyone in the damn universe better suited to Tajss than I am?

It's fine, because I'm going to beat his damn ass. I don't bother running towards him—he's coming my way anyway. I do crouch down and tighten my grip on the shock-stick, flicking its controls so that the charge in it is building to its max.

The Invader pounds the sand as he comes closer and closer. My heart pounds, my breath comes in short gasps, and fear tingles along my limbs. He's big and getting bigger as he closes the distance. Behind him, Calaun watches, yelling something, but the remaining three close on him in a mad dash.

The Invader is almost close enough. A little more. Clenching my teeth I prepare myself mentally the best I can. Hold still. Hold it. Hold… and I swing with all I've got. I aim up towards his face, hoping that it will have the most effect there.

The shock-stick connects. I hit so hard it sends an impact wave up my arm causing it to go numb. The electricity releases, pouring into the Invader's body, causing him to go stiff then shake violently.

"Yes!" I scream. "Take that, you son of a bitch!"

Warmth radiates through my body as adrenaline pumps into me. The Invader gurgles as he spasms, arcing bolts of blue electricity sparking around him. Then the shock-stick runs out of power. He should fall down. He should, but he doesn't.

He roars.

Oh, no.

I'm grabbed by four hands and lifted off my feet. I scream as I fight, kicking and struggling to break free.

5

CALAUN

The instant she screams I know it's her. My chest constricts, and my hearts pound hard enough to explode. One glance, and my blood runs cold.

An Invader has her gripped in its arms, holding her off the ground, shaking her. She's fighting, kicking and struggling for all she's worth, but the Invader is twice her size.

Memories burst from the fog of the bijass. It's not her I'm seeing but a Zmaj female. The cold in my blood is replaced by burning rage. The emptiness that comes with this memory fuels hate that's been locked away forever.

The three Invaders fighting me close. This is it.

Spreading my wings I throw my arms wide and roar. A burst of fire escapes my mouth along with the sound. The Invaders pause, a fatal mistake.

They've captured her. I won't let the past repeat.

Ducking my head I rush the one in the middle of the three, the biggest of them. My shoulder connects with his stomach and I lift up, wrapping my arms around his waist.

He's taken by surprise, air whoofing out as I barrel

forward, carrying him over my shoulder. I turn left not stopping. He pounds his fists against my back, so I slam him with my tail over and over until he stills.

Closing with the next one, I throw the now-lifeless body. The surprised Invader drops his weapon to catch the body of his commander. It's a stupid mistake. I'm on him in a flash, barreling him over.

We tangle together with the limp body, all of us hitting the ground hard. I land on top and slam my fists into his face, not bothering with technique, pure rage carrying me through.

Blood flies, but before I can make sure he's out, the haft of my own lochaber slams against my throat. The third one retrieved it and is using it to choke me out. He pulls back hard. I grab hold of the wood and struggle to keep it from cutting my air off.

I'm dragged off the two downed Invaders in a new fight for my life, but more importantly, for hers. I can't fail. Not again.

The monster has four arms locked onto the strong, flexible shaft, jerking to tighten it against my neck. My wings and tail are pinned between us. I push back into him, struggling against the loose sand and my opponent both.

He growls in my ear, his breath foul, muttering words I don't understand. I find purchase with my feet and push my way up to standing. He leans backwards, pulling me along with him, the shaft tighter.

My vision grays as my lungs scream for air. I'm blacking out.

Can't. Can't fail. Stay.

One chance.

I throw myself forward with everything I have. The shaft crushes my throat, cutting off the trickle of air. My vision is almost black, but he's pulled forward, up onto my back. I bend my knees, then thrust powerfully up and back.

We flip up into the air, falling over backwards. He lands under me, breaking my fall. I give up on fighting for control of the shaft, slamming my elbows into him as hard and fast as I can. There's a cracking sound as his body armor gives way.

The blackness is almost complete, dancing lights and shapes pass over my vision, but among them is her and I keep fighting. Slamming elbow after elbow, again and again. Another loud crack and he cries out, losing his grip.

I roll off of him onto my hands and knees, gasping desperately needed air. A foot hits me in my ribs, throwing me up into the air. Stars explode through my vision, and I can't catch my breath again. I slam down on my side. The Invader storms forward. I bring my tail around and slam against his legs, knocking him to the ground.

Throwing myself on top of him I pound his face with my hands interlaced until blood sprays and he quits moving. Stumbling to my feet I whirl around, afraid of what I'll find.

The Invader that captured Annabel slaps her with one of his hands and she stops fighting, going limp in his grip.

Red covers my vision, wiping away the pain.

He's going to pay for that.

I run and leap, wings spreading. He turns as my shadow falls across him. looking up in time for my fist to connect with his face. He drops Annabel, stumbling backwards. I catch her before she can hit the ground.

Cradling her in my arms, I turn and lay her down gently in the sand, then spin back to my opponent.

He growls, four arms with closed fists swinging as he charges wildly. I dodge three fists and miss the fourth. It slams into the side of my head. My ears ring and I stumble to the side.

I can't let this drag out. Charging, I take hits as I close the distance, but then I'm inside his arms. The dragon roars. I belch blame into his face. His hair ignites and he screams. I pound my fists into his ribs and stomach then hit him in the face while slamming my tail against his leg.

His leg snaps with a loud crack, and he drops to the ground. He struggles to rise, screaming in pain and rage. I turn and slam my tail down on his head. He goes silent.

I run to Annabel, and she's already up in a sitting position.

"Go!" she yells, pointing past me. "The girls! Save them!"

Following her arm, I see three females running from two Invaders. There's a pounding in my ears as my vision narrows. This cannot be.

Ignoring the stabbing pain in my body I run. My throat is dry, but strength suffuses my body. I'm going to destroy them.

I leap, bounding across the sands. The Invaders have technology that lets them move on the sand easily despite their large size, but this is my home. Tajss is mine.

The two males grab the females right before I catch them. Their screams cut through the pounding in my ears, but it's fuel. Fuel for the rage, feeding the red haze of the bijass.

Dim memories of the war before the Devastation drift below the fog. Barely within my awareness, but provoking further anger.

I don't hesitate as I barrel into the closest of the Invaders, leaping forward and tackling him around his legs. The move throws him forward and he hits the sand hard.

Thud.

In an instant I've climbed up and over so that I'm on top of his back, forcing his head down into the sand. He struggles wildly. Four arms flailing, legs kicking, but I push him in deeper. Let Tajss claim its vengeance for me.

These Invaders have caused too much pain.

His fighting slows, he's almost done for, when the other moves in the corner of my vision. He shifts the human to his other side and brings his gun to bear.

Dropping down, I drive my arm into the sand and around the throat of the one I've pinned. In the same motion I roll backwards, pulling the Invader with me. The shot fires, electricity crackling through the air, and the Invader I'm holding takes it.

The Invader spasms violently then stiffens. The bolt's stunning effect is minimal on me but my limbs and core have tingling sensations as if they had fallen asleep from my sitting wrong.

I let the Invader go, scrambling across the sand without bothering to rise, putting distance between myself and my opponent. He fires again and again. The crackling bolts barely miss me. They hit the sand, sending puffs of it into the air.

One hand sinks into a soft spot, and I don't move fast enough. A bolt hits my left leg and it's numb.

I have to end this. The female in the Invader's arms is fighting, keeping him from taking a true aim, but it's only a matter of time before a shot finds my center mass.

I can't feel my leg, so standing isn't going to work. I've got one chance. Pulling my wings and tail tight against my body, I hold my arms against my chest and then roll towards him.

Sand, sky, sand, sky, sand, sky over and over. I can't see him, I'm rolling on instinct, hoping I reach him before he moves.

As despair takes root that I've missed him, I see him on a roll. One more roll.

There! I kick with my good leg, landing a solid blow behind his knee. It buckles forward and he stumbles. The gun's aim shifts and it fires. The bolt lands behind me.

My leg is throbbing, but I can't let it stop me. The female screams as he violently shakes her, trying to stop her struggling. She doesn't let it slow her. She pounds her small fists against his arms and chest, kicking at his legs.

When I push myself up, my left leg won't hold my weight and buckles. As I drop, I grab onto his arm with the gun in it. He fires as I jerk it down with me.

The electrical bolt dances across the sand at my feet, making them tingle, but it doesn't make direct contact.

He fights to free his arm but refuses to let go of the gun. Good.

I let his arm slide through my grip until I reach the gun itself. Getting a good grip on the barrel and another on the stock, I twist hard and fast.

Snap!

Bones break, and he screams in pain and rage. I'm on my knees, unable to stand, so I hit the most sensitive spot I can reach. I drive my entire head up into his crotch.

The sound he makes is more a yelp than a scream, and he stumbles backwards, letting the female go. I crawl across the sand after him. He's not out, and I won't stop until he is.

He doesn't fall, managing to keep himself upright somehow. Yellow eyes glare and he hisses, showing his sharp teeth. He throws his four muscular arms wide then flexes them in and roars.

Strength rushes into my body as the red mist consumes the last remnants of rational thought. It buries the pain, so I leap up to my one good leg. The left refuses to hold my weight, but I've got two legs for a reason.

Using my wings and tail for balance, I hop across the distance between us as he rushes in. We slam together with bruising force. The only thought in the red mist is Annabel.

I see the fear on her face. Pain. As I struggle with the monster, her face melds with another. A face from long ago, one I'd let the blessed fog of the bijass claim. My heart aches recalling her, but she's gone. I failed.

I won't fail Annabel. This monster won't win. Not again.

The fight goes to the ground as we grapple one another, struggling for any advantage. I grab a handful of sand and throw it in his face, blinding him for a moment. He hits me so hard I see stars.

We're rolling over and over. Hitting, being hit, getting a grip then losing it as we tumble around. When we come to a stop, I'm underneath him. The female is screaming in terror, but I've got him where I want him.

It's a fight, but I get an arm around his throat and lock my other hand on my wrist. Pulling tightly, I arch my back and complete the chokehold.

He fights hard. Elbows pound against my ribs. My right side screams in agony, ribs there already broken. Probably they're shattering under the impacts.

Can't breathe, but it doesn't matter. Saving her. Annabel moves through my thoughts. Appearing in the red fog. She smiles, and her smile lights the world.

She's the one.

She can't be. I don't know how. No Zmaj can have two loves. One life, one treasure, that's the way it is.

It's almost as if my soul itself is being torn apart. It's a problem for later. One that won't matter if I lose this fight.

He throws himself to the side and my hand slips. I'm losing my grip. I roll with him and now I'm on his back. It gives me more room; I pull back harder. His struggles lessen.

His fists pound the sand growing weaker until at last he stills. I hold my grip for several more heartbeats to make sure he's not faking. When his body remains limp I drop and use the last of my strength to roll off of him.

Lying on my back I stare up at the suns, letting their warmth radiate through my body. As adrenaline drops away the pain flows in behind it. Every breath is a stabbing pain and comes up short. My leg is slowly regaining feeling, but it feels like someone is driving sharp objects into it repeatedly. Every part of my body is bruised at the very least.

The biggest concern is the ribs. Everything else will heal without attention. I'm going to need medical attention. I can't let that stop me, these females need to reach the City. I need to report back to the Order with what I know of this latest incursion, but the females must come first. They are part of the Vision and the Great Plan.

"You damn fool," Annabel says, appearing into the field of my vision.

Moisture drips from her eyes, rolling down her cheeks and falling on my chest. The water is cool on my scales, but it radiates a strange warmth.

"Is everyone safe?" I ask, breath hitching as I speak.

"Thanks to you," Siara says, kneeling on my other side.

"How badly are you hurt?" Annabel asks, wiping her sleeve across her eyes and stopping the falling moisture.

Forcing a smile I push myself to a sitting position. It's pure agony, white-hot pain exploding in my left side that leaves me seeing stars and gasping for air. Once I'm up it recedes, so I put the smile back.

"I've had worse," I say.

"Can you travel?" Annabel asks.

"Yes," I say.

She looks around, pursing her lips. As I watch her, memories and perception meld. Her face shifts towards that of the uncovered memory. The pains in my body don't compare to the empty ache that comes with that memory's return.

I close my eyes, focus my thoughts, and center myself in this moment. The past is gone. Now is what matters.

"Can we use their machine?" Annabel asks.

"It is... doubtful," I say, having to pause to let the pain pass. "Their machines... are attuned to their bodies."

Her frown deepens, creating a tiny wrinkle between her eyebrows as she thinks. I'm fascinated by her thoughtful expression. It casts her face with a deep intelligence that I want to know better. My heart throbs, aching with the conflict of thoughts.

"Then we have to walk," she concludes, pursing her lips.

Full, luscious lips that beg to be kissed, explored, tasted.

"Yes," I say.

"You can't walk," she observes, staring not at my face but at my chest.

"I can," I say.

"Don't be an idiot," she says, pointing at my left side.

When I look down, I see her concern. My left side is turning a deep purple, almost black color. Blood is pooling under my scales. A quick assessment from years of battlefield experience makes me sure that my lung on that side has collapsed. It makes sense. That's why I'm having such a hard time breathing and the pain isn't easing.

"Do you have epis with you?" I ask.

"Yes," she says. "A small supply."

"A small bit will help numb the pain," I say. "With it, I can walk."

She bites her lip and nods. "We'd better hurry. We won't stop now. We can't risk another fight."

"Yes," I agree.

The other females have gathered around in a semi-circle. They look at each other, then back to Annabel, but no one contests her statement.

"RaiAnne, Siara go retrieve our sled. Ella and Nina, come with me. We'll explore their transport and see if there's anything worth salvaging."

"I can help," I offer.

"You can damn well sit here and wait," she snaps. "You're hurt, and I have no doubt movement is going to make it worse. Let's save that movement for getting us closer to the City."

I nod agreement as my prime cock stiffens at her dominance. She is beautiful.

6

ANNABEL

This sucks. Every step he takes hurts. It's obvious in the way he walks, but worst of all is the sound of his breathing. He's wheezing. Every exhale from his lungs comes along with a whistling sound that literally terrifies me.

I'm pushing aside the fear as much as possible, but it's mixing with the memories of Quintin. I remember what happened to him when he was trying to protect us. Calaun is obviously not Quintin, but the comparisons are too clear not to be drawn.

The suns are sitting on the horizon, making their last fight against their inevitable drop. Long rays stretch across the sand like fingers grasping at a cliff before they fall. Fits my mood and thoughts perfectly. It's how I feel all the time. I'm clinging to a cliff and doing my best to not fall, but it's not only me on that cliff. That would be bad enough, but all the others are hanging off of me too and if I fall, we all fall.

"You should ride on the sled," I say for the umpteenth time.

"No, I'm fine," Calaun says.

Flecks of blood decorate his beautifully sculpted lips, and

when I see them a cold chill races down my spine. Internal bleeding. Great.

"It's getting worse," I say.

He stops and looks at me seriously. "Yes."

"So lie down on the sled!" I yell, blood pounding in my ears. How can he be so stupidly stubborn?

"No," he says. "We're almost there. Look."

He points into the distance. As I follow his arm, the distinctive glitter of the City dome is visible breaking the horizon. Despite myself, my heart beats faster and a sense of relief rushes through me, making my limbs shaky.

"Fine," I exhale, shaking my head. "You're still being stupid."

"Perhaps," he says, a wan smile forming on his face.

His color is bad, and he's obviously weaker than he was. The Zmaj each have distinctive coloring to their scales that accents the edges. I've noticed with Gomul that they tend to shift with the particular Zmaj's mood but not distinctively enough I've ever figured out a pattern. Calaun's colors are pale and washed out. It can't be good.

He and I stare each other down for a long moment, and he's weaving on his feet but stubbornly refusing our help. The ache in my chest throbs. I want to help him. That's all it is. Losing him would be inconvenient, a setback. He's helped us, and I'm not an asshole. That's all this is. I'm trying to be nice.

The tightening in my lower belly, that almost-forgotten stirring of something more, it's nothing. No, I'm returning the favor. He's helped us, and we should pay that back. The girls gather close, waiting for the two of us to resolve this. Their eyes weigh heavy on me, and my cheeks warm under their attention.

"We should move," I say, giving in.

Calaun nods and leads the way. Standing behind I watch

him walk away and can't help noticing the way he sways from side to side. He's obviously doing his best to hide it, but I see it.

"He'll be okay, we're almost there," RaiAnne whispers, gripping my upper arm.

"I hope so," I admit, glancing at her.

She smiles back. I take a deep breath, exhale it slowly, and then we continue our journey. Worrying about him is a good thing if for no other reason that it's keeping my mind off what's coming next.

The City. Which means Rosalind.

Rosalind is probably my least favorite person on the planet. She's arrogant and overconfident and, in my opinion, a damn fool. Meeting her again isn't high on my list of things I want to do, especially since we're coming to join her City.

My heart skips a beat. Her City. Ugh.

There's a reason I wanted to stay in the desert. Gomul and the girls think we should go to the City and become part of the larger collective. I kept us there as long as I could but eventually, I saw the inevitable future. I was losing control of them and soon they'd go whether I wanted them to or not. Like Kate.

My stomach churns pushing hot acid up my throat that I swallow down. Kate is the one who screwed this all up. If she'd been able to get along, we'd all be fine. Except we wouldn't. Quintin would still be gone.

I'm not a fool. I've made mistakes, and she was one of them. Now I'll have to handle her. There's not going to be a choice. She is here, probably. She could be at the Tribe. Though none of us have been there, we've heard of it. At least some people don't want to kowtow to Rosalind.

Except the leader of the Tribe married Rosalind. So she's got her fingers in that pie too. That woman!

My thoughts circle creating one terrible scenario after

another. It's a dark mess and I'm sure I'm going to regret having come here. Rosalind will be condescending with her air of superiority. Looking down her nose at me and mine with that holier-than-thou attitude, as if she knew all along we would bend to her will.

Gritting my teeth, I push down all the worries and focus my attention on the world outside my own head. It doesn't work completely the terrible thoughts are all bubbling right there, pulling at my attention, but it's at least better.

I didn't used to be this petty, did I? I don't think so, but on the ship everything was easier. So much easier. On the ship, I had Quintin. He could pull me out of the spiral. His smile was enough to brighten the room and when I'd get down, he'd wrap his arms around my waist, jerking me close then he'd kiss me. Kiss my face, down my cheek, to my neck where he knew it tickled, and he wouldn't stop until I was laughing so hard tears were rolling down my cheeks.

I miss him so damn much. It still hurts. It's been forever, probably two years or more, but every time I think of him the pain is there, as fresh as the day I lost him. What am I supposed to do with it? It won't go away.

Quintin was kind, gentle, and I know in my rational times that my happiness was the most important thing in the world to him. I'm not happy and that would kill him. Well, if the damn monster hadn't done it first. God, that's a dark thought.

Get out of your head, Annie!

His name for me. Anyone else who called me that would raise my hackles, but when he said it with so much love it would melt my heart. He's the only one I'd tolerate it from. The only one I secretly liked it from. I'd give him hell for it, but that doesn't mean I didn't like it. He got that.

Quintin got me.

That's what I miss. I didn't have to explain myself to

Quintin. He knew, words were an unnecessary medium. He understood me so thoroughly, so deeply, that we didn't have to talk about it. It was magical.

What am I supposed to replace that with? A stubborn alien dragon-man? What could he know of the pain I've been through? How could he possibly understand me with anything near the perfect understanding Quintin gave me? What good is any relationship that falls short of what I had?

None.

That's the answer. It's not. I don't want anything less. The universe stole my love from me and now here I am. Living this bleak and pointless life—but I'm responsible for these girls. They depend on me, and if they don't have me then they'd be lost. I'm the one who's kept them alive. Who's made sure they had food, shelter, and that they didn't do anything stupid.

Even Kate. She may have betrayed me and run off to join the other camps, but I bet she knows, deep in her heart. She wouldn't have found her new mate if not for me. The happiness she has now, that's because of me. I did that, not that I think she'd ever admit it.

She doesn't have to because I know. These girls are the only value I have left in this world. The only reason to go on. I have to take care of them. It's my duty and my responsibility if for no other reason if not me, then who? Rosalind?

I snort out loud, and RaiAnne looks over startled. Rosalind has her hands full being Queen of the Universe. What time does she have to take care of *my* girls? None, that's the simple answer. They'd be another cog in her great plan for whatever that's worth. They'd be lost in the machine. I'm saving them from that fate. They decided to come here, but I'm here to make sure they get what they're due. That they're protected and cared for and that they find some kind of happiness.

Once they do, then my job will be done. And then what?

Calaun looms large in my vision, and in an instant my heart leaps, beating faster, and a fire burns deep in my belly.

Nope. That's not it. Not going to go there.

But… nope. I close my eyes, blocking off the vision of the admittedly sexy Zmaj. This is primal. A girl has needs that have nothing to do with love. Problem is, I've been around the Zmaj enough to know that they aren't into one-night stands. There's no scratching an itch with a Zmaj. You go to bed with one you come out with a life-mate whether you want it or not.

I don't. I can't.

No matter what my body thinks it needs. I'll find some alone time and handle that ridiculous urge soon enough. Until then… the dome dominates the horizon. We're almost there, and my dislike of Rosalind and her attitude is enough to occupy my thoughts—so focus on that.

As we reach the airlock, Calaun leans against the humming barrier that protects the City. Another nicety that they have here. They don't have to hide in a hole in the ground to avoid predators. Their fancy dome keeps all those concerns at bay. Spoiled brats. Rosalind could use some time alone in the desert. Be good for her. It would test her superiority there, wouldn't it?

"Who are you?" the man on the far side of the airlock says.

"Who in the burning sands do you think we are?" I snap.

His eyes widen. He has gray at his temples, a wrinkled worn brow with busy salt and pepper eyebrows that arch up so high it looks like they'll reach his hairline. His mouth hangs open in surprise at my attitude or his inability to form a coherent sentence in response. He sputters, waves his hands, then half-reaches for the stun rifle slung over his shoulder.

"I don't... uh... know... uh, yeah, uh who are you?" he finally gets the words out.

"I'm Annabel," I say. "We're survivors too? You know, fellow humans looking for shelter. Can we get in now, in case you didn't notice, our friend here is hurt."

I try to be nice. It's hard. He doesn't seem like the brightest of people, and to be honest, the rattling wheezing sound of Calaun's breathing is stressing me out. The man looks at Calaun, and his eyebrows do that leap for his hairline again.

"Oh," he says continuing to stare. "Oh... right."

He punches a code into the small box next to the airlock and our side swishes open. We walk in, leaving our sled behind, as there's no room for it and us too. The door swishes shut behind us and warm air blows around us as the pressure and temperature equalizes. As it does, the heat index goes down at least twenty degrees, which is a welcome relief.

While we wait for the process to cycle through, a small crowd of people gathers on the other side. Arrivals must be a novelty. Great, now I feel like a circus display, which does nothing to improve my mood.

Calaun rests against the side of the airlock. He's breath is coming in short, ragged gasps that he's doing his best to hide. It sounds wet, and he's in obvious pain. Biting my lip, I try to ignore it, but I can't take my attention off of him. He's hurt, badly.

"Calaun," I say, moving in front of him.

"Yes," he says.

His eyes are glassy, and his color is pale, washed out. It looks like an effort for him to lift his head to look at me.

"We're almost there," I say. "Hang on."

I touch his arm, intending to be supportive, but there's a spark between us. His scales are cool to the touch. He gasps at my touch, his eyes lock onto the point of contact. His scales are smooth but with a texture that is unique.

Slowly he looks up from my hand on his arm until our eyes meet. Cursed time crawls past, and I know this can't be more than a moment but it feels like an eternity. When our eyes meet the weight of his gaze is too much. In this instant I'm stripped of my protective façade, and he sees me.

It's terrifying and exhilarating in the same breath. His hand moves towards my face, almost touching my cheek, then he drops it to his side. He coughs, a wet sound, turning his face away.

"I'm fine," he insists.

The door whooshes open behind us and the moment is over. Which is good. I'm about to make a damn fool of myself.

"Can we get some help here?" I bark, wheeling on my heel to face the operator and all the morons who've nothing better to do than stare at us. "In all your gawking, can't you see he's been hurt?"

The gathered crowd mutters, but two men separate themselves from the group and get on either side of Calaun, gently pushing me out of the way. He leans on them, more than I'm sure he'd like, and they help him out of the airlock.

"I'll let Rosalind know you're here," the airlock operator says.

"You do that," I say, gritting my teeth.

My group follows the men helping Calaun towards aid. The crowd of onlookers drifts back to whatever they were doing as the excitement of our arrival passes. The City has changed. The streets are mostly clear of debris. The broken, deteriorating buildings are of course the main décor, but it's clear that the place is inhabited now. It no longer has that ghost town feel.

I don't want to admit it, even to myself, but it's nice.

Rosalind has done good work here. I guess I should get used to it. This is, apparently, going to be home. If Rosalind lets me live here. If I don't go crazy under her tyrannical rule. Either of which are definite possibilities.

We arrive in the main town square with its large statue. All of us stop, and there is more than one gasp.

"Water," Nina says, saying the word all of us are thinking.

The fountain is working. That's new. All of us stare at it in wonder. The water isn't spouting up or anything like it was probably originally designed to do, but it is flowing, and it does look fresh and oh, so inviting.

RaiAnne, Ella, and Siara look at me, and I shrug, trying to downplay it. The looks on their faces make it clear that I don't succeed. Damn it.

"Did I call it or what?" Siara asks.

"You did," Ella agrees.

"Can we get Calaun some help please?" I ask. "Or we can stand here staring at the ostentatious display while he suffers some more from internal bleeding."

The girls have the decency to look abashed and we continue on, but I feel bad. I'm being a jerk for no other reason than I hate being wrong. Who does want to be wrong? Seriously. So I'm still being a jerk.

A harried woman runs out of the building in front of us. She has a stethoscope around her neck and is wearing a lab coat, so I assume she's the doctor I've heard they have here. Or the scientist who works as a doctor. Whatever. She runs right up, eyes locked on to Calaun. A Zmaj is right behind her.

"Melchior, take him," she orders.

The Zmaj steps in and sweeps Calaun off his feet, then the two of them run into the building without a word. The girls look askance at me, but I run after them. He's my responsibility. At the very least, I'm not going to be shut out of making sure he's okay. I've lost one man, I'm not doing it again.

They go through a double set of doors that swing back and forth and I follow. It leads to a set of stairs that have been makeshift repaired. A few of the steps look like they've been here forever but then others have boards over them showing big gaps around them. The girl and the Zmaj race up the stairs with the ease of familiarity. The first one of those boards I step on bends under my foot and my heart leaps into my throat as it creaks loudly.

I push past the fear and resume climbing. I keep close to the wall as I do, hoping that I'm avoiding a devastating fall by doing so. The other girls follow behind me, and we make our way up. I keep an eye ahead and see the door that they take Calaun through.

The stairway is barely lit, which doesn't help anything in here. It's like a setting for a horror vid. When I get to the door they went through, I step out onto to solid flooring and exhale in relief.

This floor is immaculately clean. An open area with a handful of chairs, almost like the waiting room of a doctor's office. Did they have such things on Tajss before? Am I projecting what I know from the ship on to the alien landscape? There's only one door they could have gone through, so I take it. As I put my hand on it, I turn to the girls.

"Wait," I order

I'm not sure why I'm telling them to wait, but it feels like the thing to do. They don't argue, taking seats. They're worried about him too. We're not fools, and all of us heard his breathing. I don't want them to be there if we lose him. They've lost enough, and they don't need to have another loss happen in front of their faces.

That begs the question, why am I going in there?

It's not a question I have an answer to. I'm drawn to him,

not that I want to admit it, and I won't if anyone asks. That spark between us calls to me. I'm curious, but I can't let it go too far. I can't forget Quintin or betray his memory, but that doesn't mean I want anything to happen to Calaun. He was nice, he saved us, and I owe him for that if nothing else.

Through the door is a laboratory slash medical facility. Long metal tables line the walls, all of them too tall for a human to comfortably work at since they're designed for Zmaj. Equipment, jars, vials, and various things I don't recognize clutter across them. There are three beds in the space with thin curtains hanging down between them. They've put Calaun up onto one of them, and Addison is moving a handheld machine across his body.

Her lips are pursed, her brow furrowed, and she looks worried as she stares at the machine in her hand. It makes clicking and whirring sounds as it passes down his body, growing louder over the area of his ribs.

"Internal bleeding," she says, setting the machine aside. She touches his side, it looks like a light touch but Calaun grunts. "We have to drain the blood."

She doesn't hesitate an instant as she reaches for a nearby tray and grabs a needle. She inserts it into Calaun's side, then sets it aside and picks up a scalpel. She pauses and looks across him at me.

"This won't be pleasant," she says.

"I'm fine," I say, crossing the last of the distance between us.

I take Calaun's hand in mine and stare into his face and eyes. I don't want to see what's about to happen. Butterflies dance in my stomach and bile tries to rise, but I push it down.

"I'm fine," he says. "Nothing to worr—"

His words are cut off as his mouth snaps shut and his grip on my hand tightens painfully. Blood spurts out of his side splashing loudly on the floor. It looks like a gallon of it flew out and covered everything in its path including Addison.

I can't keep down the bile at the sight of it. Memories flood back and I'm shaking. Quintin's blood exploding out of him as the thing bit down on him. The warmth of it splashing across us as he screamed. Turning away I close my eyes and force the memories away.

"Almost," Addison mutters.

Peeking through a barely slit eye she's sewing up the wound she created to drain the excess blood pooled there. The wound is barely bleeding now leaving only the mess behind to indicate its severity.

"That's… better," Calaun says, inhaling and exhaling deeply.

"Good," Addison says, finishing up her sewing job. She straightens, stretches her back with hands on hips then looks at Calaun. "I'm Addison."

She sticks a hand out to him and he takes it in the human custom.

"Pleased to meet you," he says. "Thank you for the assistance."

"Of course," she says. "This is Melchior. Annabel, we've met before, but good to see you again."

"Same," I answer.

"Melchior," Calaun nods.

"Order?" Melchior asks.

"Yes," Calaun answers without elaborating.

"Rosalind know you're here?" Melchior asks.

"I do not know," Calaun says.

"I'm sure she does," I say, crossing my arms over my chest and resisting the urge to huff.

As if in answer to the question there's a knock at the door.

"Come on in," Addison says.

Sverre walks in. Like all the Zmaj, he's big, but he carries an air of easy authority with him. A calmness that spreads around the room when he enters. When he walks in, you pay attention. There's a magnetism to his presence that is compelling.

"Hello," he says, stopping a few feet from the bed. "Good to see you again, Annabel."

"You, too," I say, which isn't completely a lie.

"And you are?" Sverre asks Calaun.

"I'm Calaun, member of the Order," he answers.

"Welcome, Calaun," Sverre says. "We look forward to continuing to strengthen our alliance with the Order."

"Same," Calaun says.

"Unfortunately, Rosalind and Visidion are out of the City right now, so they will not be available to welcome you and your group."

"That's too bad," I say, trying to keep my elation under control. The longer I can hold off having to deal with Rosalind the better.

"Until they return you are all welcome," Sverre says. "Though I might inquire as to your intentions. Is this a visit? A trading effort? Something else?"

He's looking at me as he speaks. I swallow hard. This is the part that I've been dreading. Saying it to Sverre is much easier than Rosalind though.

"My group would like to move to the City," I say. "Calaun happened across our path on the way and kindly escorted us the rest of the way. He must speak for himself on his intentions beyond that."

"I see," Sverre says, nodding, but his attention has gone to Calaun.

"I'm along for the ride," Calaun smiles. "My duty will require I return to the Order soon, but as you can see, I'm a bit slowed down on that."

He motions to his newly stitched side. His color is returning, but he's still pale, and his breathing remains shallow, too. He'll need some time to heal, but even so, he swings his legs off the edge of the bed and sits up.

"Slow down, cowboy," Addison says, putting her hands on his shoulders.

"Thank you, it's much better, and I will take it easy, but I'm fine," Calaun says.

"Of course," Sverre says. "How did you come to be so wounded?"

"We had some… adventures," he says, looking at me. "The last one was a run in with the *Invaders.*"

The way he calls them that, he puts an emphasis on it that doesn't fit. It's as if that's not the name he would call them by, like he's bowing to a local convention and not what he really thinks. He knows something he's not saying. I'm sure of it. It's in the undercurrent of the conversation and the tension that falls over the room as he says it.

"Invaders?" Sverre asks. "How far out?"

Calaun answers the next several questions, and I'm grateful he's there for it. I have no way of measuring distance on this planet. What would I say? Oh, you know, twelve dunes to the south? Even the dunes shift in the constant breeze that moves the sand slowly from one spot to the next.

When they finish, Sverre nods. "Thank you. I need to gather the Council and discuss this with them."

"Good idea," Calaun says. "If they have any questions, I'll be happy to answer."

"Good," Sverre says. "Annabel, make yourselves at home. If you truly wish to stay here, please find Bert. Ask around for him. He will assign you to duties as appropriate to your skill sets. All that live in the City contribute—it is all we ask in return."

"Fine," I say, gritting my teeth.

It's not all they ask. They also expect you to kowtow to Rosalind the High and Mighty, but I'm not going to make waves. At least, not yet.

Sverre takes his leave of the four of us. Addison checks over Calaun while I take a seat on the next bed. Melchior stands on the opposite side of Calaun from me, arms crossed, watching it all. He's got that same look in his eyes when he watches Addison work. That gaze of devotion, dedication, of love.

Quintin looked at me like that. I miss him so much. Quickly I wipe away the tear that falls, but not before Calaun notices. He doesn't call attention to it, but his eyes are warm, caring, and full of understanding.

"I should see to the others," I say, sliding off the bed.

"You know where to find Bert?" Addison asks.

"No," I admit.

She gives me directions, and makes me repeat them back to be sure I've got them right.

"He'll fix you up," she says. "We've gotten a lot of the space more livable now. He'll make sure you and your girls have someplace nice to stay."

"Thanks," I say, walking towards the door. As I pass by Calaun, I pause and look at him. He's watching me, quiet and thoughtful. "Thank you."

"You're welcome, of course," he says, his voice soft.

"We…" Part of me hates saying this out loud, but I have to. "We wouldn't have made it without you."

He smiles but shakes his head. "You are an extraordinarily strong female. I have no doubts you would have figured something out. I merely aided."

Addison's eyes are dancing back and forth between the two of us, so I need to stop this before she gets any bright ideas that there's more here than meets the eye.

"Still, it's appreciated," I say, turning and walking the rest of the way to the door.

"I'll be around," he says. "If you need anything."

Hand on the door I pause, trying to think of something clever to say. When nothing comes to mind, I try to think of anything to say, but when I come up blank, I decide, screw it, and walk out the door without answering.

7

CALAUN

My stomach sinks as she walks out the door. Silent, strong, willful, yet tempered with intelligence and self-awareness.

Where does she fit into my life? When I saw her in danger, my memories of before returned as fresh and raw as when they were created. That Invader grabbing her gave me flashbacks to before the Devastation, when the war was nearing its inevitable end, and I lost my love.

My mate was captured in much the same way as Annabel was, only that time long ago, I wasn't fast enough. I didn't save her. I failed.

When the bombs dropped, destroying everything, I wandered the empty wasteland, lost. Alone. Filled with nothing but my own regrets and a death wish. The bijass that came on all of us after the Devastation ate the past, and I welcomed it.

When I was found and recruited into the Order, it gave purpose to my empty life. A reason to exist, some semblance of sanity to the insanity that I only dimly understood was our past. The Order was reason. I needed its structure, and I still do.

No Zmaj has more than one mate in a lifetime. I know that as deeply and truly as I know that my dragon is claiming her.

It's a conundrum. I do not understand it, nor do I know what I'm supposed to do now. I'm drawn to her. Her fire warms me, calls to my soul, the dragon needs it to reignite the fires of my own passion. Yet, I can't. It is impossible.

"Are you okay?" Melchior asks.

"Yes," I say, not looking at him.

"Addison," Melchior says. "Could I have a moment with Calaun?"

Addison looks up from the work she is doing at the table beside us. Her eyebrows rise in surprise, but she snaps her mouth shut and nods. She walks out of the room without another question or comment.

"Brother," Melchior says.

He uses the word broadly. Our records on the people of the Tribe have documented the way they use most terms in their culture. The Order has been collecting information for lifetimes. There is so much to learn inside our walls, but we must keep all of it secret. Hidden, in case those who would destroy us get their hands on it.

Our enemies are legion, and our only defense is to hide. True for all of Tajss. If the Invaders carry word… No, I won't let my thoughts go there.

"Yes?" I ask, focusing on Melchior.

He doesn't speak for a long moment, staring into space as he formulates the words he wants to say.

"You won't win," he says at last.

"Win?" I ask, confused.

"The dragon will claim what it wants," he says.

"I'm fine," I say, understanding what he's referring to now.

"No," he says. "You think you are, but you're not. You won't be, until you accept it. She looks at you in the same way. Anyone who sees you can feel the connection, the attraction."

I frown, unwilling to look too closely at this. My emotions around it are not clear. Indeed, they're a turmoil of noise that I don't know how to handle. So I won't. I'm going to focus on my duties, which right now means getting healed enough to return to the Order.

"Thank you for the advice," I say. "I'll keep my own counsel on this matter though."

Melchior frowns, shakes his head, then turns, and walks to the door. He pauses and glances back.

"You can try, of course, but don't break her heart while you do it. The dragon won't be denied."

He walks out the door leaving me alone. I watch the door swing back and forth, brushing its mate as it does. My side hurts and it's hard to get a deep breath. Memories surge against the fog of the past. Giving in to all of it, I lie back on the uncomfortable infirmary bed and close my eyes.

The dragon stirs in the depths of my soul. It's laid a claim that I don't know how to possess. Annabel. Of course I'm attracted to her. She's strong, smart, and beautiful, why would I not find her attractive? That doesn't mean I can claim her as a mate though.

My duty to the Order, for one. There are no females in the compound. When the humans come to visit, we restrict their access. We don't even let the other Zmaj know all we have at our disposal. Secrecy is in the very nature of what we do. As I've progressed through the ranks I've learned more and been given a deeper and deeper understanding.

Our purpose—no—our calling is so much higher than

considerations on one male's mate. It's not about me or even those of us alive right now. It's about salvaging the planet. The Devastation was a reset. A needed one. We've made the ultimate sacrifice in losing all we had and all we were. That's a responsibility I can't set aside lightly.

The future of every living being, not only on Tajss but in this galaxy, depends on what we are doing here. The survival of both of our races. There won't be a second chance. The entire galaxy would descend into a dark age the likes of which would make the Devastation look like child's play. We can't let these Invaders and outsiders gain control of Tajss again.

My thoughts drift along as sleep slowly creeps over me. My last thought is of Annabel. Her smile and brilliant mind and she is leading the charge against the Invaders, defending Tajss.

8

ANNABEL

"So the meals are fairly regular, though we stagger serving times because of space mostly," Bert says.

He's a nice enough man, but tedious. We don't have work assignments yet because he needs to coordinate them with the other teams. He is giving us a tour of the City and proudly showing off the improvements. It's a lot nicer than it's ever been before.

"All the meals are served communal," he continues. "You come in here and there will be tables set up with stuff. It changes all the time, we like to keep it fresh. Some variety is the spice of life, right?"

"Variety?" Ella asks, perking up.

"Oh yes," Bert says. "We trade with the Tribe for their vegetables. Our hunters get a lot of different meat. We've got a lot of seasonings we salvaged from the ship, too."

"Salt? Oh my god, please tell me you have salt!" RaiAnne all but grabs the older man by his shoulders and shakes him.

"Yeah," he says, rubbing his forehead. "We sure do."

"You are my hero!" RaiAnne exclaims. "Do you know how long it's been since we've tasted salt?"

"Uhm, no, I'm sure I don't," Bert says uncomfortably.

"Too long!" RaiAnne says, dramatically waving her arms around as if she's about to faint.

"All right," I say, voice sharp.

They know I don't care for the theatrics. Everyone is doing their best to survive. The girls exchange a quick look, but they shut up. I know I piss them off, but they need to behave. We're guests here, and I'm sure Rosalind will get reports about us and how we act.

"Well, it is about mealtime," Bert says. "Are you all hungry?"

We all agree we are, so he leads us to the dining hall. When we arrive, there are a handful of other humans in the area, already at tables eating. They sit in small groups along the long tables. It's clear that they've been breaking down into their own little cliques. Well, we'll have to form our own.

Those gathered look at us in a not unfriendly or unwelcoming way, but they also don't go out of their way to make us feel at home. I don't really expect anything different, but it would have been nice. If Quintin was here, he'd be making friends already. He was good at these things. Social interactions were his strong suit. Anytime we'd go to a gathering or a party, he would be fitting right in, while I would be the girl in the corner, watching it happen around me.

I bet Calaun would be at home here too. His easy, confident swagger as he walks in the room would have all these people eating out of his hand. I wish I could be like that but that's not me. People are hard. They don't make sense. They expect things they don't say. They want things from you all the time.

"This looks amazing," Siara says, leading the way across the room to the table that has the food laid out on it.

"Thanks," Bert says, as if he's solely responsible for the

food and its presentation. “We work hard on it. Try to make the best of our life here, ya know?”

“It looks like it,” Nina says.

We all get plates and fill them full. There is a huge variety of food compared to the meager rations we’re used to getting by on. My biggest fear is that my eyes are much bigger than my stomach. I want to try all the different things, even though I don’t know what most of them are.

We pick a section of the table for ourselves and sit down. Bert joins us, which is nice, I have to admit. He’s not leaving us on our own, and I appreciate that.

I’m about halfway through my plate, all of us too busy eating to take time for small talk, when there’s a commotion outside the door. Suddenly the door slams open, banging against the wall, causing all of us to jump.

A streak races through the door followed by another. They’re moving so fast I can’t make out who or what it is. It’s small, two to three feet tall, but other than that it’s a blur. The blurs race for the food and then a voice calls after them.

“Illadon! Rverre! SLOW DOWN!”

Calista. I recognize her voice but that must mean those are the babies. I drop my fork and it hits the plate with a clatter that’s covered over by the crashing sound as one of the babies crashes against the food table. The table tilts up on to two legs, barely balancing. The food slides, heading for a fall, then the table shifts back and slams onto all four legs. The food is jostled but nothing is lost.

The entire room breathes a sigh of relief.

“Did you see that!” a small, yet masculine voice yells.

Illadon is holding the edge of the table, pulling it down to rest on its legs. He’s small but much bigger than the last time I saw him. He must be close to three feet tall, and for a toddler, he’s muscular. He’s shirtless, like all the Zmaj, wearing loose flowy pants. His chest is covered with scales and the first hints of abs. His biceps bulge as he pulls down on the table. Tiny horns protrude from his forehead, and his hair is long, dropping past his shoulders. He's got the most adorable smile I've ever seen.

He's not talking to the room though, he's talking to the other small Zmaj next to him. She's standing beside him with her arms crossed and a frown on her face.

"I did," she says. "I'm not impressed. I did better, I stopped *before* I hit the table."

That must be Rverre. She wears a rather plain dress with a rope belt around the waist. Her hair is even longer. With curls dropping across her back and covering her wings, it reaches the top of her tail. She has scales on her cheeks that are a flushed-looking shade of pink. She waves a finger at Illadon.

"Your mommy is going to be very mad," she says.

"Nah," Illadon argues.

"Yes, I am," Calista says walking into the room at last. She looks hurried but she has a smile on her face. "Good job, Rverre. Illadon, you could learn a thing or two."

"Ah, mom," Illadon says, "she should learn from me. I'm strong!"

He spins on one foot, wings flapping, tail waving, and comes to a stop with a full-on bodybuilder pose. Rverre snorts.

"I'm faster," she says.

"Wanna bet?" Illadon asks.

"No!" Calista barks. "It's food time. Enough of the antics."

"Yes, mom," Illadon says, his attitude changing on a dime.

He smiles at Rverre, grabs a plate, and then carefully picks out what he wants to eat. A perfect gentlemen emerging from the wild child that tore into the room. Rverre returns his smile and follows suit picking her food. Calista walks along behind them, filling a plate until they reach the end of the table. When she turns and looks out across the room, her eyes land on my group. She walks to us without a hint of hesitation.

I like Calista, but I don't necessarily trust her. She's firmly in Rosalind's camp, which means she's not firmly in mine.

"May we?" she asks, nodding at an empty seat across from me.

"Of course," I say, and the other girls give their assent.

Small talk breaks out immediately between Calista and the girls. I only half-listen, because Illadon has most of my attention. I can't quit studying his tiny features. He's grown, a lot, but now I can see the human influence on him.

Sure he's got scales, horns, wings, the whole nine-Zmaj-yards, but Calista's input into his DNA is clearly written on his face. Especially there. The soft, full roundness of his cheeks and his nose exactly duplicate hers in miniature.

The color of his hair is dark like hers too. Mostly there is something about him that screams of his mother. His eyes, I think. They're remarkably similar to hers in shape and set. As he eats, his tiny fingers tear at the pieces of meat. He has tiny nails that extend just far enough to be claws, but it's not overly pronounced.

Once I've fully studied every detail of every scale on his precious face, I move my attention to Rverre. In her it's similar, but Jolie is of course a much different woman than Calista. Rverre has her mother's almond eyes but her nose is her father's. It fits her face well, and it's clear she will grow to be a beautiful woman.

Her horns are much less pronounced than Illadon's. Barely small nubs protruding past her hair and ending in blunt points whereas his curl back along his head. I wonder if all Zmaj females have smaller horns? It wouldn't be unprecedented, at least according to what I recall of old nature vids that Quintin would watch.

He never wanted to stop learning. He was fascinated by life and all it had to offer. Fascinated to the point it killed him. He's gone, and maybe if I let him go, I could have something new. I could have a baby.

We talked about it often enough. We even started trying, for a while. It hadn't been very long by the time we had all the paperwork necessary for it done back on the ship. Obviously, it hadn't been long enough since I never did end up pregnant.

My womb throbs with emptiness, pulling out hormones that set my thoughts on fire. A baby. A beautiful, perfect baby to fill my days. Perfect scales and tiny wings.

"Is that your opinion, Annabel?" Calista asks, cutting through my thoughts and jerking my attention back to the table.

"Hmm? Oh, uhm, yes," I stumble over my words as I rush to catch up with the conversation happening around me.

The look on everyone's face makes it clear I've said something monumentally stupid. Heat rushes through my face making my ears burn. Nina clears her throat pointedly.

"I think what she means is that she thinks it's a bad idea too," Ella says, covering for me.

"I'll say what I think of what," I say. "I wasn't paying attention to the prattle, what are we talking about?"

My girls look embarrassed at my handling but Calista smiles. "I get it. We're talking about the fact that Gershom is gone, and now we're trying to build bridges between those who followed him out of actual belief."

"So, what's the question?" I ask.

"If you feel that there should be a separation between Zmaj and humans," Calista says.

"No!" Illadon says, leaping out of his seat, wings flapping furiously to lift him, and he lands on the table. He crosses his arms over his chest and stamps his foot, tiny claws on his toes scraping against the metal. "That'd be stupid. I'm half-human, what would they do with me? Or Rverre?"

"Illadon, get down," Calista says.

"You show me who thinks that way, I'll show them!" Illadon declares, holding up a fist.

"I won't ask you again," Calista says. "Standing on the table is rude. You must stop it."

He jumps off the table and lands on his chair. He sits down with a harrumph, but then Rverre pokes him in the side and the two of them engage in a game of poking one another.

"Of course I don't feel that way," I say. "If not for the Zmaj we'd never have survived. Those who feel that way are afraid, that's all."

"Maybe, most of them," Calista says. "Yet there is still a significant number of them, even if they aren't as vocal without their leader."

"What are they doing?" I ask.

"Oh it's nothing much," Calista says quick, too quick. "Annoyances, that's all. Graffiti here and there, posters, that's all."

"That's more than nothing," I observe.

"It will be fine," Calista reassures us. "We've definitely got bigger fish to fry right now, though I'd like to handle that problem. There are a lot of problems I'd like to solve, like how to get air conditioning!"

"At least it's cooler in the dome," Siara says. "Beats the desert."

"True," Calista says. "I don't know how they manage it at the Tribe. Epis is great, but hot is hot, even if you're adjusted to deal with it."

"Too true," RaiAnne agrees.

"What other problems?" I ask, keeping the conversation from straying back into the pointless.

"Invaders," Calista says. "That's the big one. We haven't had much trouble with the Zzlo but the Invaders are a problem. Their attacks are random, without rhyme or reason. We go a long while without an attack, then suddenly there's an army of them."

"They've attacked the City?" I ask.

Calista nods. "And the Tribe."

Pursing my lips, I frown and think about that. "Any idea what they want?"

"Addison thinks it's all about the meteorite glass," Calista says. "They showed up more or less together which makes it a solid argument."

"Makes sense," I say.

"Yeah, but it doesn't give any insight about what to do about it," Calista says. "That's what we're working on. I think Rosalind might have some insight she's working on though."

"What a surprise," I mutter.

"What's that?" Calista asks.

"Nothing," I say, shaking my head.

"Anyway, that's where we're at," Calista says. "I'm glad you've decided to move here. We can use the help for sure."

"Thanks," Siara says and the other girls give their agreement.

I remain silent. I'm not glad to be here. Dread coils in the pit of my stomach, still waiting for my first encounter with Rosalind. Only after that's over will I know if I'm going to even be allowed to stay. Why would she welcome her greatest rival? Only time will tell what's going to happen, but I'll deal with what comes up as I always have. One thing at a time.

9

CALAUN

I'm past due back at the Order, but I can't leave yet. No, that's not honest. I could but I'm not going to. I can't bring myself to leave yet, and my injuries give me a good excuse to stay longer. So I do.

Longer and longer. Several days pass as I recuperate under the human female's capable hands. I could easily travel the second day, and she knows it. She doesn't call me on it, though she does give me permission to travel the City at my will.

It doesn't take me long to track down Annabel. I don't approach her at first. She's been assigned a work detail, along with the rest of the females who traveled with her. Once I find her, I watch and debate, jousting with the dragon.

Primal instinct, rational thought, and ingrained tradition war with each other, and I'm left in the middle, unsure of what the right course of action is. There are too many moving parts to this. If I choose her, the Order is never going to let her stay in the compound with me. I'd effectively be removing myself from the Order.

Or maybe not. They didn't so that to Archion and his

brother, though they don't live in the compound any longer. They are still members in good standing and check in. They're making it work. so perhaps it's not as big a problem as it seems.

That doesn't answer my memories though. The empty ache in my arms and heart that once was filled by another. One I lost. One I failed. An image breaks free of the fog, and I'm holding my lost love in my arms as her life slips away.

Pushing off the wall I'm leaning against, I suppress the memory with the same action. I'm not going to let the past rule the now. The Order is creating the future. Knowing the past does not make one a slave to it.

"She's pretty," a voice says from behind me.

I spin on my heel, pulling my lochaber as I do. Another Zmaj stands in front of me, but his gaze goes past me towards Annabel. The dragon roars, pumping hot blood through my veins. I'll tear his eyes out for looking at her. A rumble slips out of my throat as I suppress the urge to give a battle cry and attack.

I don't know this male, but he's bold. It's also a sign of how lost in my own thoughts I was if someone, anyone, could slip up on me without my being aware. It's not a good sign. The male shifts his gaze to me, his eyes darting to my lochaber then back to my face.

"You don't need that," he says, frowning.

Staring, I slowly lower the weapon and then slide it back into its straps on my back.

"Who are you?" I ask.

"Ladon," he says, simple but without offering a hand in peace. "This is my City."

"That's a big claim," I observe.

The moment he said his name, I know of him. The City was his, before the humans crashed. We knew he was here, but had written him off as too far lost in his bijass to be a worthwhile recruit. So we let him be. He shrugs at my words and ignores them.

"How long are you staying?" he asks.

"I don't know yet," I say.

His eyes gaze past me again, and I don't have to turn to know he's looking at Annabel. "I see."

"What is it you 'see'," I ask.

He returns his gaze to me, his frown deepening.

"A dragon having laid claim," he says. "Yet you fight it."

"What I do or do not do, isn't your business," I say.

"No, but this City is. What do you know of the Invaders?"

He switches topics fast, but not to one that's any better for me than the previous one, though this one is less personal. I glance over my shoulder and see Annabel looking in my direction, wiping sweat from her forehead.

"They're erratic," I say. "They attack out of nowhere with no apparent pattern."

"Yes," he agrees, and I move, walking around the corner so Annabel won't be staring. I'm too acutely aware of her gaze. "So it would seem, but there's more here than meets the eye."

"What do you think then?" I ask.

This is good information. The Order will want to know how much of the truth the City has figured out.

"I think they came along with the falling of the meteorites," he says, but it's clear in the phrasing of his words he knows something more he's not saying yet.

"And?" I prompt.

He stops walking, so I do too. He stares up at the sparking dome overhead for a long time, not speaking. I wait, patient. A silent male invites information.

"Once this city was great," he says. It's non-sequitur, but he's thinking something.

"Once, before," I agree.

"I... remember," he says, but there's an uncertainty to the statement. "Or I think I do. Some of it. It's still... hazy. Unclear, but there."

He drops his gaze from the dome overhead back to me. I nod, trying to encourage him to say more.

"Okay..."

"The space port," he says. "It was here. The main one, if my memories are right. Outside the dome, do you recall this?"

"I don't recall much from before the Devastation," I lie, but he nods, accepting the untruth.

"Most of us don't," he says. "Their attacks center, as far as I can see, around the City and the Tribe's cave. The Tribe is our source of epis. The City is the original shipping port of epis—my memories on this are clear. It's epis. The meteorites are a cover."

"An interesting theory," I say.

"It's not a theory!" he yells, hands balling into fists and scales coloring with instant rage.

His tail is straight up behind his back between his wings and he leans in towards me. I don't react, gazing into his eyes, watching, and waiting. Any sign of motion and I'll dodge, but if I respond in kind to his anger, I'll provoke him further. That wouldn't be productive for me.

When I don't respond, he finally relaxes, unclenching his fists, and his tail dropping to the ground. He shakes his head, probably trying to clear it.

"I understand," I say. "What proof do you have?"

"Proof?" he asks. "Instinct. Insight. What more proof does a male need to protect what is his? My son lives in this dome. These Invaders are a threat to him and my mate. We've lived at the mercy of their random actions, but I'm done with that."

"I see," I say. "So what is it you're asking of me?"

"I want the Order to lend their aid in a counterattack," he says.

Mentally, I'm rocked back. It's not one of the scenarios we had hypothesized and accounted for. Since the Invaders offer no central location to attack, we hadn't given any consideration to the City's deciding to launch a counterattack.

"How would you do that?" I ask.

"I've been watching the night sky," he says. I wait for him to say more, again, but he doesn't elaborate.

"What is it you see there?" I ask.

He stares with hard, judging eyes. There's a moment where it's as if he's staring directly into my heart. It's intense, but I meet his gaze unflinchingly.

"Look," he says at last. "See for yourself."

"We need to destroy them at their source," he says.

"How are you going to do that?" I ask.

I've said the wrong thing. I can see it on his face, clear as the suns in the sky. Suspicion narrows his eyes and furrows his brow. I'm not sure why that question was too much, but it was.

"That doesn't matter," he says, cutting off that line of questioning.

"I can present your idea," I offer. "I'll need to know more of the how though."

His eyes narrow but he nods. "Good. It is all I ask. There must be a solution. Will you attend a Council meeting with me?"

That is a lot further than I want to go, but at the same time, an opportunity to be in their meeting, especially when they're discussing a counterattack, is an opportunity I can't pass up. Also, it gives me further reason for not returning to the compound on time.

"Yes," I say. "When?"

"Rosalind and Visidion should be back tomorrow," he says.

"Okay, so they'll meet then?"

"They'll want to brief the Council on their trip to the Tribe," he says. "They will call for a meeting, I'm sure."

One night. I'd hoped for more. Ladon grips my shoulders with both hands and squeezes tightly. A familiarity that I didn't invite, but I can't say is unwelcome. He has come a long way from the lost soul that he was before the humans. The grand plan marches forward, and it seems he has a role to play in Tajss's future.

"Okay," I agree.

"One more thing," he says, not letting go. "Tell her. Do not fight it. Trust me, your instincts in this are good. She's rough on the exterior, abrasive in many ways, but beneath that rough exterior is a delicate flower that needs to be nurtured."

My scales itch, and the urge to walk away is so strong that I take a step back, but he moves with me.

"I am undecided," I concede.

"I know," he says. "Do not be."

He squeezes tighter, lets me go and walks away. I'm left with my thoughts. His words confirm where I was going anyway.

The Order is creating a new future. One unshackled from the chains of the past. Before the Devastation, Tajss was a very different place. A thin veil of society laid over a barbaric culture that was destroying the planet. That was the past.

Acknowledging this doesn't lessen the love I had, but the love I had is gone. I am here, now. Life is in my today and we create tomorrow. How do I want to live that future? Alone? Ignoring the empty ache as I lie in an empty bed?

Is that what my barely remembered lost love would want? Is it what I would want for her if I were the one gone?

No. I would want her to love again. I would not doom her to a life alone.

I march back to Annabel before doubts can assail my newly gained certainty. I stride towards the work detail she's been assigned to. There are seven humans working with her, hauling debris out of a building, and piling it onto a sled. I assume one of the Zmaj males will be coming by to haul it off to a dumping ground.

Three males stop working as I approach. Annabel walks out of the building, carrying an impressive load for a human female, and dumps it onto the sled. She grabs a skin of water and takes a drink, that she chokes on when she sees me walking up.

She sputters the water, then wipes her mouth with the sleeve of her blouse. I stop an arm's length in front of her, smiling.

"Annabel," I say.

"What?" she snaps, looking from me to the gathering workers watching us.

"I would like to ask you to dinner," I say. "Tonight. Will you share water with me?"

Her eyes widen as her cheeks color a soft pink. She stares into my eyes then her attention darts to our audience. I don't care they are watching, but I do pick up on the signals that she does, for some reason. Do these humans not respect mating rituals?

The humans whisper to each other, watching. I wait, patient. If she turns me down, it's fine. Right now I want to explore the idea of the two of us. I don't know if this is real myself, no matter the urgings of my inner dragon. I need to get to know her better. I want to see if there is more here or not. If she turns me down, I'll do that in some other way.

"What do you mean, dinner?" she asks.

"I would like to get to know you better," I say. "I thought, perhaps, sharing a meal would be a good way to do this."

Her eyes narrow, her lips purse, but she nods. "Fine. Dinner, but that's *all.*"

She emphasizes the last word, and two of the males watching suppress laughs.

"Of course," I smile.

"I will get you after your duties are complete," I say, giving her a partial bow.

I turn and leave without another word. I've got work to do if I'm going to make this a special event for her. A song that I barely remember comes to my lips, so I whistle it as I make my way to the mess hall for supplies.

10

ANNABEL

Why did I say yes? I'm insane. I can't do this. I've got nothing to wear, for one.

Ugh, what does it matter what I wear? I'm *not* interested. I'm *not.* He put me on the spot, that's what it was. Everyone was looking at us. Here I am trying to find my place in this new world order, and he springs this on me!

Is he nuts? Am I?

My sleeping quarters look like a hurricane hit them. I've tossed my meager belongings all over the place as I've tried to decide on what to wear interspersed with decisions to tell him I'm not going. Collapsing on to the makeshift chair in the corner, I stare at the mess.

Nothing. I've got nothing to wear. Unfortunately, the clothes that survived the crash have long since been worn to nothing. Everything I do have is threadbare, tattered, and or stained beyond any hope of actually being clean. Sooner rather than later I'm going to be down to wearing furs that we harvest from the damn beasts.

Do they have clothes production in the City? I hadn't even thought to ask. They might, actually. It's not like I have a clue how to make clothes. You go to the store, you buy them. That's how you get clothes. I know someone had to make them, but that wasn't my problem on the ship. It wasn't my job to do.

A soft, pinkish shirt rests on top of a pile next to the small pallet I call a bed. I grab it off the floor and hold it up for inspection. It's not too bad. There's a dark stain on the back-left side that I've never been able to get out. Bivo blood, if I recall correctly. Okay, well this is the best I've got.

What am I worried about? This isn't a date. I'm only doing this to say thank you for helping us get here. That's it. Nothing more. I'm sure he's not worrying about what to wear. Zmaj males have it easy, they only wear loose pants that all look the same. His entire choice is do I wear my brown pants or my brown pants! It's not fair.

And it's not a date. Nope. No how. This is *not* a date. I'm not going to notice his overly defined abs or the bulging muscles of his arms. Or the fullness of his lips and the deep color of his eyes. My stomach tightens, aching, and I'm acutely aware of the void between my legs that hasn't been filled in so awfully long.

If the Zmaj were different. If they believed in one-night stands, then maybe this would be more than not-a-date. They don't. I know this for a fact, and I'm not going there because of it. I'm not going to commit myself or get a Zmaj stuck to me because I have an itch to scratch.

I run a hand over my stomach that's not nearly as flat as it used to be. I'm not fat, we didn't have enough food for that, but I'm softer than I was, despite the harshness of the life we've been living. I'm getting older. I'm not a young girl anymore. The big three-oh has come and with it my body is going through changes, but it hasn't dulled my basic needs or desire. Desire I haven't scratched in a long time. I don't recall the last time I had any time to myself.

Idly, I move my hand over my mound, pressing on my full soft lips. I shudder at the pleasure of the sensation, which encourages more, begs for it even.

Closing my eyes I stroke my hand across my pussy, soft touches, barely opening the pink lips. Mostly putting pressure onto my hooded clit, letting the sensations build slow. It feels so good. My heart speeds up, making me a little lightheaded, so I check the door and my privacy, then move to the pallet.

I lie down and run my hands over my tits, grabbing and pulling at the heavy flesh, teasing the nipples. Working my way down my body, I rub my hands over my sides and stomach, enjoying the smooth feeling as my skin slides underneath my touch.

Down my thighs, then slowly dragging my hands back up towards my core. I squeeze my legs together, applying pressure to my clit then drive my hands into the wedge of my legs. I spread my legs and run a hand over my now-wet pussy.

I give it a light slap, and I gasp in pleasure at the sudden change in sensation. Laying my hand flat I rub hard until the tingling sensation reaches new heights. I pull up to my breasts, squeezing and working them, until my nipples are hard and erect.

Moving back down, I hold my lips apart with my left hand and use my right middle finger to rub up and down my opening. Teasing the clit and my opening with an almost penetration. I bite my lip, my back arching involuntarily.

"Mmm," I moan softly. "Uh-huh."

My imagination runs wild as pleasure takes over from rational thought. It's no longer my hand working my pussy, but a strong, masculine man. I'm bucking with pleasure, thrusting my hips forward as I demand more. Deeper.

Fingers penetrate into my soft, wet folds. Pushing in

towards my core. Big, strong fingers. More than manly fingers. Zmaj fingers.

It's not a man, it's Calaun. He has big hands, massive fingers. Each one close to the size of a human's cock. I bet they'd feel so good driving into me, like this. Deep, in and out, pushing and pulling.

He'd curl them inside me, finding the magical spot. Rubbing. Like this. Yes!

"Oh!" I moan, biting my lip to keep it from being too loud.

He works his fingers in then he pushes in two, forcing my pussy to expand and take his girth. My mouth aches, I want to taste him. Feel his big cock on my tongue, pushing back into my throat. I push my fingers in as the illusion of my imagination continues to play.

I'm bucking and thrusting on the pallet. On one level I know it's my own fingers pushing in and out of my pussy, but the fantasy is fresh, exciting, and getting me off.

I want his fingers, I want his cock, I want him to ride me.

I rub my clit with one hand and keep driving three fingers in and out with my other. The soft sound of skin on skin echoes to my ears as I finger-fuck myself towards an orgasm. I turn my head and bury my face into my pillow to muffle the sounds.

I bite down. I'm close, so damn close. Suddenly it grips me, and my body tightens as an orgasm rips through. My toes curl, and in its aftermath, even my hair is tingling.

Damn that was good. I lie on the pallet panting and exhausted by the force of the release. My heart racing, pulse pounding in my ears, breath coming in short ragged gasps. I should get up but instead I lie here naked letting the aftershocks work their way out of my system.

As the last of my orgasm passes, I'm immediately self-conscious. Sitting up I pull my clothes and crush them against myself. What am I thinking?

Crossing the room I go to the small wash basin and clean up, doing my best to cleanse myself of any hints of my pleasure. Then I don't bother picking anything special to wear, but grab the cleanest, nicest looking blouse and pants I have and put those on.

The sheets of my pallet are a jumbled mess, reminders of what I did. Frowning, I straighten them up, then clean the room by putting all my scattered clothes back into packs. Once it's clean, I survey the space, then go to the small window and look out. The suns are dropping in the sky, but I'd guess I've still got some time to kill before Calaun arrives.

Great. Time to kill. What do I do now?

When I sit down to wait, I realize that extra time is the one thing I try to avoid. I prefer to be busy. Doing something, anything, because when I've got time on my hands all I do is think. Think and remember.

I hate thinking too much. I hate remembering even more. What good does it do me to remember? Almost I could be jealous of the Zmaj and their loss of their memories. All they're good for is hurting you.

Such as the last things I said to Quintin. The way we argued, and how that's the last thing he would remember of me, of us. I didn't want him to go out, but he had to, or so he thought. He didn't. He shouldn't have. If he'd listened to me, then none of the bad stuff would have happened.

Now I'm here. Alone. Except I'm not. Calaun has a fire in his eyes and I hate to admit it, but I like the way he looks at me. The way I feel when he looks at me. There's a soft knock on the door, and I jump.

I walk to the door, hesitating with my hand on the knob. Biting my lip I compose my thoughts and face, then open the door. Calaun is standing on the other side. He's smiling, dominating the space of the door. He's a big guy. Broad shoulders, muscles all over his chest and stomach. He fills the opening physically but more than that, he takes my breath away. The strong lines of his jaw, the rich color of his eyes, his hair is a touch long, soft-looking and inviting. A small part of me wants to run my fingers through it to see if it is as soft as it looks.

"By Tajss…" he exhales, his eyes looking up and down me.

Warmth rushes across my chest and onto my cheeks. I can't meet his eyes. He's got that look on his face again.

"Hi," I say, shifting my weight.

"You are… stunning," he says.

"You're… ridiculous," I counter, shaking my head. I can't let myself fall for his words, though my body betrays me, warming and aching with desire and needs.

"No," he says. "That I am not."

He steps to one side and offers his arm to me. I step out and take it, pulling the door shut behind myself. He leads the way down the hall. It's a wide hall. The buildings are designed by and for Zmaj, so everything is too big from my perspective. Doors, hallways, ceilings, all bigger than average, or what I'd expect.

Many of the doors we pass are open to let the air in or out. People inside of them stop and stare as we go past. The sounds of their voice grow silent until we move beyond their sight. Some of them come to their doors and stare after us as we walk. I had no idea we'd make such a spectacle.

He leads the way outside and through the City. The suns are low, causing shadows to stretch across the streets. The City is cast in shades of amber and red as the light of the double suns fights its way through the protective dome. It's pretty in a post-apocalyptic kind of way. Since it's close to dinner time the streets are mostly empty with only a few people out and about. Even now, life is finding a way.

Calaun takes us a few blocks away then enters another building. We carefully climb the broken stairs, and he never lets go of my hand as we do. It's easy for him to step over the missing or partially broken stairs, but more of a challenge for me to do. He helps though, considerately, letting me work it out myself the best I can, and only helping when I ask or accept. It's a small thing, but I'm glad for it.

When we reach the top of the stairs, he leads us through another hall and across open rooms until we emerge onto an open-air terrace. A low wall surrounds the open space. In the middle is a blue blanket with a box sitting on one corner. Small mismatched pillows are laid out along each side.

Calaun stops, steps to one side, and motions at the blanket, giving a half-bow as he does. I can't stop myself from smiling. My throat closes and tears well in my eyes. It's sweet. He's watching me as I take it in, so I swallow hard, feeling the need to acknowledge this somehow.

"Wow," I say, shaking my head and blinking away the pooling tears.

Quintin did something similar once. It was at one of the massive parks back on the ship, laid out under a tree. It was wonderful, a magical day that we often talked about later. How could Calaun have known that? He couldn't have, of course.

"I hoped you would like it," he says.

"I do," I agree. "It's very nice."

"Come!" he says, taking my hand, and gently pulling me forward.

He kneels onto the blanket and digs into the box, pulling out plates that he sets at my feet and in front of himself. I kneel too, using a pillow for comfort. He pulls out smoked meats, dried rations from the ship, and a small container of what looks like fruit.

"I wasn't sure what you would like," he says. "So I acquired as much as they would allow."

"Thank you," I say, looking from the spread of food to him. "It's very sweet."

"It's nothing more than you deserve," he says.

He's waiting for something more, but I don't know what to say, so I grab a piece of the smoked meat and pop it into my mouth. As I expected, it's very chewy, giving me cover while I figure out what to say.

"You didn't have to do this," I say. "But I appreciate it. Will you be leaving soon?"

"I'm not sure," he says.

He eats some meat himself, and we chew in silence. Strangely, it's a comfortable silence. That's something I hadn't expected, or experienced in years. The suns drop lower and the first stars appear in the sky while we eat. He makes small talk, and I do my best to be engaged with it.

"I've never been good at this," I say at last.

"And what is 'this'?" he asks.

"Small talk," I say, smiling. "Dating. This."

"Dating?" he asks, arching an eyebrow.

"You know, when a boy and a girl go out to see if they like each other," I say immediately regretting that I opened my mouth.

Why did I say that? I'm not dating him!

"Fascinating, tell me about this 'dating,'" he says.

"Zmaj don't date?" I ask.

"I don't think we did," he says, looking past me into some foggy distant past "Perhaps? Tell me about it so I can answer better."

"Well, it's like," I trip over my own thoughts as I try to figure out how to break down the idea of dating for him. "Usually someone is interested in another person. They think they might be cool, or maybe they think they're in love.

You can't know for sure though, not until you, you know get to know each other. Does that make sense?"

"No," he says smiling. "How can you not know you love someone?"

"Love is complicated," I answer.

"No, love *is*," he responds.

"Sure, but that doesn't mean it's like magic. It's a thing, yes, but how could I know I loved a man unless I really knew him?"

He sits up as his brow furrows, and he shakes his head.

"Because you've always known them," he says softly.

"What? That doesn't make sense," I say.

"A Zmaj knows," he says. "The moment we lay eyes on the one, we know."

"No way," I say. "That can't work every time."

"It does," he insists. "Because it is true. Love is truth, love is a binding that stretches across time, always. One soul knows its kindred."

"That sounds like a romance novel," I observe.

He smiles. "Perhaps."

"You're serious?" I ask.

I'd thought he was pulling my leg or something. If he weren't a Zmaj, and I didn't know anything about them, I wouldn't have thought anything more of it than he was trying to get into my pants. Something on his face says there's a lot more here though. He shrugs.

"Would you like some of the fruit?" he asks, lifting up one of the bowls and offering it to me.

"You're changing the subject!"

He stares at the small bowl in his hand, refusing to meet my eyes.

"Perhaps," he says.

"Now you have to tell me," I say, leaning closer.

He sets the bowl down then looks into my eyes. The

double sun rays are blasting their final attempts to not be swallowed by the horizon. It causes lights to dance in his eyes like tiny furnaces alight with fiery passion.

"I do not wish to be forward," he says.

"Then you shouldn't have mentioned it," I say.

"True," he says. "Very well."

"Good, now tell," I encourage him. "What is it you believe?"

"We Zmaj are native to Tajss. The life of the planet pulses in our veins, it is part of us. It manifests in different ways. The bijass, you know this term?"

"Yes," I tell him, and he nods.

"It is a part of it," he says. "A piece of Tajss herself. Many of us call it our *dragon*. That part of our soul that is ancient, instinctive. It is the voice of Tajss talking to us."

"Sounds… primal," I say.

"Yes," he agrees.

"But that doesn't explain love. How can you know you love someone you don't know?"

He smiles and nods. "Tajss knows her own."

"What do you mean by that?" I ask.

He frowns. "Each of us is our soul, but we are only part of who we were created to be. Each of us is half of a soul really. A male needs a treasure. Someone or something to protect. The other half of his soul."

"Love isn't always between a man and a woman," I say.

"No, though that was rare, it's not unheard of," he agrees.

"I'm sorry, go ahead," I say. "I didn't mean to interrupt."

"The two halves they call to each other," he says. "When a male lays eyes on his other half, he knows it. The dragon lays its claim. It's instant, there is no need to 'get to know' them because he does know them. He's always known them."

"Oh," I say. It's big and scary and too much like blind

faith. I've never been one for believing anything blindly. "So it's fated?"

"Fated?" he asks, thinking about it. "No, not really. It's... less demanding? Less insistent? If I cut apart a piece of wood, the two pieces fit together naturally. This is no different. They were one soul split into two bodies. That is all."

"Then how do you explain the Zmaj falling for human women?" I ask. "That falls apart right there. How could the split 'souls' be torn across an entire galaxy generations apart? What kind of sense does that make?"

"I don't know," he says softly.

Silence falls between us as we're both lost in our own thoughts. It's a crazy idea, and obviously one based on some deep mythology. None of the other Zmaj have mentioned this before, and while part of me finds the idea appealing, rationally it makes no sense.

"Well, it's a nice idea," I say.

"Yes," he says simply.

We gaze at each other. I don't know what to say and he doesn't seem to have anything either. The last rays of the sun drop far enough that we're cast in shadow. Wouldn't it be nice, to find a new soul mate? Could I?

What if my soul mate wasn't Quintin? We were great together, but I never considered him as such. I loved him, very deeply, yes, but it wasn't love at first sight. Suddenly I'm hyperaware of Calaun's presence as my attention goes back to him.

He's so... there. Imposing, demanding by his very presence that I pay attention to him. Briefly, my thoughts flit to my moment alone in my room earlier, and my cheeks flush. I'm instantly wet. I can smell him, the distance between us is small. I'm drawn toward him like gravity pulling the planet around the sun. He pulls me in by force of personality.

We move closer, inch by inch. I don't know if either of us

is in control, or if we're obeying some long-forgotten primal command. I'm barely aware of the passage of time as our bodies drift in each other's orbits.

Almost together. My lips tingle. Desire to taste his mouth pushes me closer still. He raises a hand and brushes the hair back from my temple. I shiver at his touch. I promised myself I wouldn't do this. The entire point of my interlude earlier was to take the edge off and make sure I didn't do something stupid. Unfortunately, if anything, it only made it worse. An appetizer before the main course.

And what a course he is. His fingers wrap around the back of my head and he pulls me closer. Still we're not kissing, but his sudden act of dominance turns me into putty in his hands. I want him. I want him to take me. Don't leave the decision up to me, take it and take my body and make me his.

My lips part, my tongue darts to moisten them. His forehead touches mine.

"I don't understand it," he says, voice husky and deep. "But you are the one."

"Take me," I say.

Rationality is gone. It's the dumbest, worst possible thing I could say, and it's absolutely the one thing I want the most.

He doesn't hesitate. His lips crush to mine as he jerks me onto his lap. His hands are all over me, and I'm touching him all over in return. This isn't nice, gentle lovemaking. This is flat-out fucking.

Desperate with need and desire, we fight the clothes off of each other. Cloth tears, but it doesn't matter. We need to be naked, now.

I need fucked.

His cock is rock hard, springing to freedom and bouncing as I finally get his pants undone. My shirt falls off and my pants are half removed. He lifts me by my hips, moving me over his erection.

It's huge. Scary big. But I'm so wet that the head slides in easily. He pauses, holding me there as his girth forces more room inside me. As I slide down his hard shaft, the bony ridges tease my clit as they slip past it and into my depths. Each one causes me to shudder as it passes, which forces his cock deeper.

We don't stop touching, kissing, moving our hands everywhere on each other as his dick drives its way home. When he is fully seated, I wrap my hands in his hair and pull tight.

"Claim me," I whisper hoarsely.

"Mine," he growls, slapping my ass. Then he lifts me up and drops me back down.

His dick pulls out and drives back in. I'm lost to the pleasure of it. I get my legs are under me and take over the speed, and I fuck him like there's no tomorrow. Fast, hard, in and out, I claim him even as his dick lays claim to my desperately wet pussy.

He grabs my tits and fondles them, teasing the nipples then nibbling on them. He grabs my hair, jerks my head back and roughly kisses my throat.

"Whose are you?" he growls.

"Yours," I cry out as he bottoms out inside of me again.

"Mine," he says.

Suddenly he rises to his feet, keeping me impaled on his massive cock. He turns around and then gently lays me down on the blanket.

His body engulfs me. He thrusts in and out, and I cry out my pleasure. He grunts with each thrust, and it drives me wild. I want more. Deeper, harder, and he delivers.

He fucks me like there's no tomorrow, then suddenly he drives in hard and holds. As he does, a fresh orgasm clenches me, my muscles contracting. My back arches, and my toes curl as he explodes inside of me.

He holds himself deep inside, but still our juices leak out

and down my leg. As the intensity of the moment passes, and his eyes focus back on me, something shifts in them. He slowly pulls out, and instead of lying next to me and cuddling, he moves back to sit at my feet.

"I'm sorry," he says. "I did not mean to… I let my passions consume me."

I sit up and reach out, touching his face. "It's fine."

He meets my eyes, and we gaze at each other in that awkward post-sex moment. A one-night stand between two people who will definitely be seeing each other again. Passion spent, but now what?

"You're okay?" he asks.

"Yes, of course," I say. "It's fine. I needed that too."

He nods. "I will not enforce my ideals on you. I did not mean to, it was not my intention."

"Good," I agree, touching his face and letting my fingers trail along it. "I'm not ready." His lips purse and his frown deepens. "Yet."

When I add the last word, his eyes jerk to mine, widening, and his mouth opens. He doesn't speak. Closing his mouth, he nods.

I've given him hope. I mostly mean it. Now that the afterglow is fading, I feel guilty. I betrayed Quintin. I haven't been with any man but him in a really long time, but he's been gone so long I barely remember what it felt like for him to touch me. And I need to be touched.

On one of our last days together, Quintin was urging me that I should keep living if something happened to him. I never thought, then, that it would. Even here on Tajss I thought everything would work out, somehow. Until they didn't.

Live Annabel. For me, keep living.

I don't know if he had an idea of his fate or not. I also

don't know how he would feel about cross-species sex, but then that's a conversation we never got to have.

"Annabel," Calaun says, touching my face and pulling me from my thoughts. "My dragon knows. I know, in time, yours will see it too."

My heart stops and my breath catches in my throat. No pressure, but he just laid claim to me in a whole different way than shoving his dick into me.

Great, I've really put my foot into it this time.

11

CALAUN

Annabel's question consumes my thoughts. If the dragon recognizes its claim because it sees the other half of itself, then how is it that the Zmaj males are finding their mates in human females? The Eye had predicted long ago that the alien humans would arrive here. It was core to the Order beliefs. It was the future hope that kept us strong through the Devastation and doing what we had to do.

Now it's here, but I'd never put the idea into balance with the older beliefs. The understanding of our very nature, the predator from which we evolved into a civilized race. Our inner dragon. Could the soul be thrown across the vast space between Tajss and the humans' home?

The truth is, I don't know, any more than I understand how my dragon can lay claim to Annabel. I had my mate. While my memories of her and that time are hazy and mostly covered with the fog of the bijass, I do recall it was real. It was natural. Exactly what it should have been.

So how can I have *two* other halves of my soul—that aren't me? Am I a third of a soul? And if so, then will Annabel and I still be incomplete?

These philosophical questions swirl around my mind as I walk through the City only half-aware of my surroundings. I don't have the answers to any of my questions. Every question I come up with only leads to more questions. It's frustrating, but as I cross the plaza to the main building, I have to put all those questions away.

Duty calls and that is higher than my idle wonderings as to the nature of love. Carefully packing away my thoughts, I focus as I enter the building and make my way up to the Council Chambers. When I approach the large wooden double doors I run into Ladon.

"Good, you made it," he says.

"Yes," I say.

"You still agree with me, right?" he asks.

"I cannot speak for the Order," I say carefully. "I will listen though, and report to them with my recommendations."

"Good."

We walk into the room together. A large table dominates the center of the room with stools around it. I recognize every person in the room from files we keep on them at our compound, though I've never met them in person.

Rosalind and Visidion stand side by side at the head of the table. They're attention is on a map laid out before them. As I walk in, Visidion points at it and moves his finger in a circle.

"Yet they're not only centered there," Rosalind says. "They've struck at the mining settlement too."

"Yes," Visidion agrees. He picks up a marker and places it in another spot on the map.

"There's no rhyme or reason to their attacks," Sverre says. "Which means they're after something we don't see yet."

"I agree," Astarot says.

Rosalind looks up as Ladon and I let the door close

behind us. Her eyes subtly narrow, and the smallest of frowns plays on her lips.

"Hello," she says. "You must be Calaun."

She walks around the table towards me with Visidion in tow.

"I am," I say. "It is an honor to meet you, Lady General Rosalind."

Her gleaming white space leathers creak as she holds her hand out. I take it in mine in the human custom and shake it.

"I don't suppose you have more insight into these Invaders," she says, studying my face.

"I don't," I shake my head.

"I have an idea," Ladon says, not hesitating.

"What is it?" Rosalind asks, returning to her position at the head of the table.

"We need to drive them off the planet," he says. "Strike back in a way they'd never expect."

"Such as?" Visidion asks.

"A missile," Ladon says, and dead silence falls around the room.

"Great, where would we find such a thing?" Rosalind asks.

"I have some ideas," Ladon says, staring at the map.

"You're serious?" Astarot asks.

"I am," Ladon says.

"Even if we had a missile, which we don't," Astarot says. "How would one single missile take out anything with any sort of certainty?"

Ladon frowns, then a fiery-haired female stands up excitedly.

"EMP!" she exclaims.

"What about EMP, Amara?" Rosalind asks.

"Look at the pattern," she says pointing at the map. "They hit here and here and here, plus we've had sighting of them in other places. The only way they can cover that much ground is to have a base in space."

"I could see that," Rosalind agrees.

"Right? So if they have a base in space, then we hit that base with an EMP and bam, we know we can take it out, shields or no shields," Amara says.

"What is an EMP?" Astarot asks.

"Electro-magnetic pulse," Amara says. "It will scramble anything electrical or electronic."

"Won't their shields protect them from such a blast?" Visidion asks.

"No—well, ours on the ship wouldn't have," Amara says.

"All of that is very well, but we don't have a missile or a way to create an EMP that would be sufficiently big enough to make a dent in this."

"We do," Ladon says.

"We do, what?" Rosalind asks.

"Have a missile," Ladon says.

"How do you know this? Have you been holding out on us?" Visidion asks.

"No," Ladon answers. "I haven't, but I have been researching and digging through the old books and scrolls we've come across."

"What does that have to do with anything?" Visidion counters.

"The space port. Draconov was once the biggest port on the planet. It also had a naval base located not far away. It was a prime defense point for an invasion," Ladon explains.

The other Zmaj in the room exchange looks, as if seeking confirmation of his words from each other. I sit in silence, waiting to see what happens.

"If it is out there, where is it? No one has run across any remnants of it," Shidan says. "We should have seen it by now."

"I wondered that," Sverre says. "It would have been a

prime target during the Devastation. Perhaps it's been destroyed."

"I do not think so," Ladon says. "Not all of it."

"What does this matter? If we don't have it, we can't pursue your idea," Visidion says.

"Could there be remnants that we haven't found?" Rosalind asks, placing a hand on Visidion's arm.

"I think so," Ladon responds. "My memories are vague, but I believe that part of the base was underground. If so, that part may still be out there, buried in the desert."

"Where?" Rosalind asks.

Ladon walks over to the table and looks the map over, then points. "There."

He speaks with absolute certainty. I move closer so I can see where he's pointing. He's scarily accurate to my own recall of where the base was. It's not something the Order has had interest in, or reason to investigate. They'll want to know this is happening.

Unfortunately, that means my stay here is growing shorter than I would like. I don't want to leave Annabel here, but I don't see that I'll have a choice.

"Does the Order know anything of this?" Calista asks, entering the conversation for the first time.

"Not that I'm aware of," I say, choosing my words carefully.

Out of the corner of my eye, I see Rosalind frown and her brow furrow. She's watching me closely, leaving me wondering if I gave some tell that I know more than I'm letting on.

"It bears investigation," Rosalind says. "Ladon, can you take charge of this?"

"Of course," he says, satisfaction beaming from his face.

"How was the trip to the Tribe?" Sverre asks.

"Good," Visidion says. "They are prospering, though there

have been more random attacks there than we have had here."

"The Tribe caves are a central focus point for the Invaders," Rosalind says.

"Is it epis?" Astarot asks.

Silence falls over the room as everyone becomes interested in the table before them. The Zmaj seem to be having memories return. Epis is the lifeblood of Tajss. Once it was the life of the universe, until the Devastation ended those times.

"What is it about epis that it is such a problem?" Amara asks. "It tastes terrible, why does everyone want it? If you live here, sure, it's the only way we survive, but why would others want it?"

"Epis was the cause of the war," Visidion says. "It led to the Devastation."

A storm rages behind Rosalind's eyes.

"What I'm about to tell you does not leave this room." She looks at each of us in turn, then her eyes stop on me. "I'm going to ask you to leave."

"I understand," I say. "I would ask that I be allowed to stay. The Order is your ally. As such, I'd like to be fully briefed that I may carry that information back to my brethren."

Her hard eyes bore into me, and I'm sure she's going to deny my request when Visidion lays his hands on her shoulders. She relaxes under his touch and he leans down to whisper in her ear. She frowns, then nods.

"Fine," she says. "When Visidion and I were off-planet, we met a Zmaj."

"What? Who? Really?" disjointed responses meet her statement from around the room.

It's information I did not know. I don't know that anyone

in the Order knew this. How would we? This is powerful information.

"Yes," Rosalind continues after the outcry dies down. "He stayed specifically to try to avoid the other planets realizing that life was still existing on Tajss. They believe it's an uninhabitable wasteland."

"But the Invaders and the Zzlo," Shidan says.

"The Zzlo are the reason that anyone off-planet knows we are here," Visidion says.

"And we fear that the Invaders are but a first wave of attacks," Rosalind finishes his thought.

I'm trying to watch every person in the room at once. They know a lot more than anyone in our ranks thought they did. This is definitely going to require me to journey back to the compound. An empty ache forms in my chest as I think about leaving Annabel behind. But I can't travel with her, even if I wasn't concerned about the welcome she would have at the compound.

"All the more reason we should find whatever we can to destroy them," Ladon says, slamming a fist on the table. "Blow them all into the suns."

"Ladon," Sverre says.

"I agree," Shidan says. "We have to act now!"

"I can't let those sons of bitches get near to Malcolm," Amara says.

The room is in chaos. They're yelling over each other, angry, scared and ready to fight. Rosalind takes a step back from the table, crossing her arms over her chest. She doesn't intervene though, instead she watches, letting the argument continue.

Sverre argues for patience and consideration. Jolie and Calista oddly back him. Astarot seems to be on the fence because he argues both ways. It's a shouting match with no end in sight.

"Enough," Rosalind says.

She doesn't yell or even raise her voice but the tone of it cuts through the noise. In a moment everyone is silent, chests heaving, hands clenched and ready for battle, but quiet. They stare at their leader, and now I see the power she wields.

A simple word. Soft spoken, but that was all it took to retake control of the room. It hits me that she did that on purpose. She let them argue, let them yell. She was letting them vent their emotions, and when she judged they had done so, she called the room to order.

It's a brilliant display of leadership. My respect for her grows by leaps and bounds.

"We don't *know* anything yet," she says, stepping back up to the table. "We suspect. We have theories. We don't have a certainty, and we don't have a plan."

"So what do we do?" Sverre asks.

"We get a plan," she says. "That means information. We need to know more. Visidion and I didn't see any creatures like these Invaders when we were on the gladiator planet, but those who came back with us might know more than we do.

"We investigate. We gather information. Sverre, you talk to Mesto and Cenar. Shidan, you talk with K'sara and Todd. Ladon, you're in charge of finding this military base. If anything is left of it, we're going to need the resources, whatever they might be.

The energy powered phaser guns that we salvaged from our ship are draining. Soon we'll be facing the Invaders superior tech with nothing more than your lochabers."

"That's enough for me to take them out," Ladon growls.

"One on one, yes," Rosalind says. "A squad? A battalion? It won't work no matter how much heart you put into it. It all raises more questions, too. Why haven't they attacked in force? How is it we keep beating them back if they have superior tech to our own? It doesn't make sense."

"You have your assignments," Visidion says. "Get to work."

The group files out and I fall in with them until a hand falls on my shoulder, stopping me.

"Would you remain behind, please?" Visidion asks but it's clear it's not a request except out of a sense of decorum.

"Sure," I agree.

In moments it's only the three of us left in the room. The two of them stand side by side watching me, but it's Rosalind who holds my attention. She and Annabel are nothing alike in appearance, but the similarity between them is striking. It's in their bearing and in their eyes. They both have such intelligent eyes.

"You know something," Rosalind says without preamble.

"I know many things," I offer. "I'm not sure what you're referring to in this case."

"I'm not interested in word games," Rosalind says.

"I assure you, I'm not either," I say.

"You reacted when I said we'd been off-planet," Rosalind says. "You reacted again when I mentioned we met a Zmaj off-planet."

She's sharp. Thoughts racing, I try to create a cover story on the fly.

"Yes," I agree. "Was I not supposed to be surprised by this information?"

"Yes," she says. "But your reaction wasn't surprise. It was something else." She turns and walks over to the map. "I also noted your reactions to Ladon's information on the base. You knew it was there."

It's a statement, not a question, and not one that I see any reason to deny.

"I do recall it existing, though I don't have any new information to give on it," I say.

"Does the Order?" she asks.

"I do not know," I answer truthfully.

"Find out," she says. "Our partnership has been decidedly one-sided. I need that to be balanced out. You can keep your secrets, but I do expect a more open flow of information on these Invaders."

"I will convey your thoughts," I say.

"Please do," she says. "This threat isn't going away, and I'm thinking they're here for a lot more than the meteorite glass."

"Was there anything more I could do for you?" I ask.

"No," she says, giving me a non-verbal dismissal.

I take my leave but now my mind is racing in a dozen new directions. Still, the one thing I want more than anything else is to see Annabel.

It's strange, the situation we're in. I need to sort it out. I know what my dragon is telling me, there is no denying that feeling. Yet by all I know and believe, it can't be, for more than one reason. The mystery of her only makes her more attractive. There are layers here to be unwrapped and explored.

And now my time to do it is limited. I must report back to the Order, and soon.

The suns are high in the sky, and I hope that she might be at lunch still, so I head for the dining area. When I walk into the space, she isn't there, but one of her companions, Nina, is. I go to her table and she looks up with a smile.

"Hey!" she says.

"Hello," I say. "I was wondering where I might find Annabel?"

"Oh, she got stuck with another detail today," Nina says.

"I'm sure she'll blame Rosalind, though I can't imagine Rosalind took the time to give a dirtier detail to Annabel."

"Where is this detail?" I ask.

She tells me how to get to it, and I take my leave. When I get to the area that Nina described, I don't see any sign of Annabel or any other people at all. I'm standing on a corner between four towering buildings. The area was bombed in the Devastation and the buildings are mostly frames with barely more than the skeleton of their forms left. The streets are covered with debris and random trash, and there's a particularly foul smell in the air.

I turn a circle staring down each of the streets and listening. After I've made a full turn, I still don't see anything. Listening carefully, I notice a scraping sound, then there's a grunt I recognize. I follow the sound and find my way across a pile of debris and then a drop down a slide of dirt. The sound is coming from this sub-floor area.

"Damn it," Annabel curses and then grunts.

Something scrapes loudly, and then her form appears in the pool of light. She's hunched over, pulling at something that is still hidden in the shadows. She straightens, stretches her back, then reaches into the shadows again.

"I will help," I offer, stepping onto the slide of dirt and rock.

The moment I put my weight on it, the pile gives way, and I'm falling. I spread my wings and try to grab air, but there's no room for them. I manage to hit my head before I slam onto my back and slide down the dirt and end up in a heap at her feet.

"Oh!" she exclaims as I fall, but as I climb to my feet she laughs. "I'm… I'm sorry that was… the look on your face!"

I laugh too. I can only imagine, but I can't be angry. It's the first time I've heard her laugh, and it's a beautiful sound.

"I imagine I looked ridiculous," I say, laughing, though not as hard as she is.

Moisture runs down her face and her skin is turning a light shade of purple as she gasps air between bouts of laughter. She's covered in dirt, smudges of it on her face, coating her clothes and her arms. This place is filthy, and it seems she is here alone.

I let her have the moment. It would seem she needs it. Slowly she is down to chuckling and trying to wipe the moisture from her face and eyes, though it leaves behind trails through the grime on her face.

"Are you okay?" she asks.

"I'm fine," I say. "I wanted to see you, but how come you're working alone?"

"Rosalind is back," she says without rancor. "She doesn't like me, so this is my penance."

"I see," I say, though I don't. The idea angers me, but I don't want to give myself over to that emotion. My time with her is limited by my looming need to return to the compound. I don't want to spend these few moments in anger.

"It's fine," she says, pushing away the last of my own anger with her acceptance of it. "I expected as much, and worse actually."

"I will help," I say. My eyes have adjusted to the dimmer light of the space, and I see she was dragging a heavy piece of debris. I grab it and lift it easily. "Where?"

"Over here," she says, leading the way up the pile of dirt.

I walk with more care this time, testing the ground before committing my weight to it. We emerge into the brighter light, and she leads the way to the corner where a makeshift sled waits for the debris. I drop it onto the cart, and we return to the work.

"I will be leaving soon," I say.

"Oh," she says.

"I did not want to go without saying goodbye," I say.

She doesn't speak for a little bit. We work in silence, but it's not a comfortable one. She's upset and thinking, but not sharing her thoughts.

"Will you be back?" she asks at last.

"Yes," I say with certainty.

"Okay," she says.

"Do you want me to return?" I ask, carefully choosing the words.

I told her I would not push, I would wait for her to know for herself what my dragon has already claimed, even though I don't understand it. She stops working and stares off into the shadows. I watch as she chews on her inner lip before she finally turns and looks at me for the first time since I told her.

"I was married," she says. "Mated. I had a mate."

"I see," I say. "You say… had."

"Yeah," she says, and the moisture is glistening in her eyes again. "He died."

"I'm very sorry," I say, but this explains so much.

She shakes her head and grabs another piece of debris, hauling it up the hill. I grab an armload quickly and follow her. The silence continues between us, and she's not looking at me again. I don't know what to say to make this better.

"The Council here is developing a plan to deal with the Invaders," I say. "I need to present the information to my brethren in the Order."

"They are?" she asks, stopping again and looking at me.

"Yes," I say.

"Great," she says, but there's a note of disappointment to her voice that I don't miss.

"What are your thoughts?" I ask.

She shakes her head. "What difference does it make what

my thoughts are? Do you think anyone really wants to hear them? What do I know? I'm not the almighty Rosalind, am I? I didn't come down in the right piece of wreckage, so I'm not on the vaunted Council!"

"I'm interested," I offer.

She stops her tirade, hands dropping to her side, mouth hanging slack. She stares, then she laughs. "You're serious?"

"Yes," I say.

"I think we need to quit reacting," she says. "But we don't have the equipment to handle them easily."

"Right, how would you handle that?" I ask, not only probing her thoughts because I'm impressed, but giving her a platform to express herself on.

"A trap," she says. "We know they keep showing up in certain areas. It shouldn't be that hard—with the right data—to figure out what they're most likely after. We lure them in, then close the door on them. Smoke them. Beat them down so hard that if any do survive, they won't think about attacking us again."

It's a solid plan. I'm impressed, and it's more doable than hopefully finding a rocket, rigging up an EMP burst out of spare parts, and getting it past their ship defenses. I can't tell her all that part though, not yet.

"That's a smart plan," I say.

"I know," she says. "But am I sharing my plan with those in charge? Nope, I'm down here in this dirty basement, hauling crap."

"Perhaps I could put in a word," I say.

"Don't you dare!" she yells, whirling on me. "I'll earn my own way. I'm not asking you for anything. You got that?"

I hold up my hands palms out and take a step back. "Of course."

She glares for a moment longer. "Good."

We return to work, and I wait for the tension to drop away before I speak again.

"Tell me about him," I say.

"Him who?" she asks, wiping her brow on her sleeve.

"Your mate," I say.

"Why?" she asks.

"Because I would know the man who won your heart," I say.

Deep wrinkles form between her eyebrows as her face tightens and her eyes narrow. Her jaw tightens, and she watches me.

"What's your game?" she asks.

I start to answer but stop myself. My answer is not thoughtful but defensive. Her question is legitimate and deserves an honest response. What am I trying to do?

The empty ache in my arms, barely recalled memories of the love I lost, a female whose face I can't recall. All I do know is I loved her. She complemented me, we were good together, and I know what I feel for Annabel is the same. Impossible but it is.

"I'm not sure," I admit at last. "You deserve a truth, but it's not a truth I have to give."

She nods accepting my answer.

"You thought of something though," she says.

"Yes," I agree. Do I tell her? Honesty has gotten me this far. "I too had a love before."

"Oh," she says. "Who was she?"

"I assume you are aware of the bijass?" I ask.

"Mostly," she says. "I think. I've picked up enough to have a basic understanding of it."

I smile. "That's probably as much as any of us understand it. It's like a fog in my thoughts. While my memory is fine overall, the past becomes a blur. Maybe it's this way for your species?"

"Well, we do forget things," she says. "I don't know if I'd call it a 'fog' though."

"I see," I nod. "For me, and others I've talked to, it is a fog. It slowly covers over memories and sometimes, something will trigger a dim recollection. A knowing I've seen something before or felt something. There's no memory connected with it though. It's an empty memory."

"Like déjà vu?" she asks.

"I do not know this word," I say.

"It means something like knowing you've seen something before but not having a memory of it because you haven't actually seen it. Or that feeling."

"Very similar then, I would say."

"Okay," she says.

"The bijass, for all of us that I'm aware of, has taken away everything of substance from before the Devastation. Some of us suffered more in the aftermath than others. The longer we're alone, the more we regress towards a primal state."

"That, I am aware of," she says, and I nod.

"After the Devastation most of us became very territorial," I say. "The survivors would fight each other on sight, defending their territory. It was a terrible time and those who were alone regressed the most."

"And you lost your… love… before the Devastation?"

"During the war that led up to it," I say. "Though I only recalled that recently."

"How recently?" she asks.

I pause, debating if the truth is the best thing to say here or not.

"When the Invader captured you," I admit. "I recalled something similar. The way you fought, even though you had no chance, you didn't give up. You were going to go down in battle. That's the moment I knew."

"You knew?" she asks, her voice soft.

"I knew you were the one," I say.

"But I'm not the first," she states.

"No," I say.

"And in your theory of one soul, two parts, this is impossible," she says.

"Yes," I admit.

She nods silently and sits down on the ground, staring off into the distance. She pulls her knees up to her chest and wraps her arms around them.

"I don't know about your theory," she says. "It doesn't make sense to me, but then what do I know?"

I take a seat next to her, close, but not too close. She doesn't react, so I take that for acceptance of my distance.

"Truth? I don't either," I admit. "It's what I was taught as a child, I think."

"I was taught differently," she says. "But..."

She trails off, but her eyes lie heavily on me, studying my face. She doesn't speak or finish her thought for a long while. I wait because I must, but my scales itch with desire to know what she intends to say. I want to know her thoughts. I want to be closer to her.

"I like the idea of it," she finishes the thought at last, and I exhale a breath I didn't know I was holding.

She reaches her hand out and I take it in mine. We don't speak, sitting here in the midst of the ruins of a once-great city. We're surrounded by dirt, debris, and wreckage, but I wouldn't trade this moment for anything.

12

ANNABEL

I'm going to do what I must. I know that Rosalind is punishing me with these terrible jobs. It's fine. I'll endure whatever she wants to dish out because I'm better than her. It doesn't matter if anyone else sees it, I do. I know it.

Calaun coming to visit lightened my mood. A lot. More than I want to admit to myself, but when you're all alone with your thoughts, what else is there to do but be honest? I like him. He's great. I like the way he looks at me. It makes me feel beautiful and special.

I like him, and my god, he was great in bed—but then there's Quintin. My stomach roils as I pull at the collar of my shirt.

Quintin.

I miss him. Every day I think of him. His smile, those bright shining eyes. The way he'd do anything for me.

Did I love him?

I don't know.

What was love back then? Someone who took care of you? Someone who was there for you? Calaun's idea of a single soul being split in two, finding your perfect mate, was that Quintin?

No. I'm going to be honest with myself, and he wasn't. I loved him, yes. Loved him in that way of depending on him. Being comfortable with him. He was great. I cared about him so deeply that I could call it love, but it wasn't *magical*. It wasn't *transcendent*. It wasn't what I sense in Calaun.

There, I admitted it. Happy with yourself?

When Calaun looks at me, my heart stops. He takes my breath away, and not because he's so damn sexy, but because he's him. The way his eyes drink me in, the way he seems to breathe me in, the way he acts. Everything about the man makes my skin tingle.

I thought it was sexual. A passing desire, that urge to scratch and get the hell over it, but now that we've done that too, it's more clear than ever that this is a lot more than an urge. When he came to see me earlier today and we sat there, holding hands, neither of us saying a word? That was the most perfect, beautiful moment I've ever experienced.

So where does that leave me? Is he my soulmate? My fated one?

Romance vids and old stories would tell me he's the one. That all I have to do is run into his arms, and then everything else will be fine. All the problems, all the difficulties will fade away in the glorious burning light of our love.

Romance vids are a joke. I grunt as I lift a particularly heavy piece of debris. My muscles burning and quivering, I haul it up the slope to the cart. I should have accepted his offer to stay for the rest of the day, but then I'd be opening myself up to… what? Letting him know I like him? Or that I need help?

I don't even know. I'm being weird. He needed to go. If they're going to try and do a counterstrike against the Invaders, then he needs to get the Order on board. Although if they do the plan he mentioned, they're stupid. Way too many ifs in their plan. As if anyone is going to ask me.

The suns are dropping below the buildings, so I end my work and head to the dining hall. I'm filthy and starving. It's a hard decision which to do first, wash or eat. I could go either way, but my stomach grumbles loudly, and it's not like I haven't seen other filthy people in the dining hall. Decision made, I head that way. This way, once I'm fed, I can wash and go to sleep. This work sucks.

The dining hall is buzzing with conversation as I walk in. A lot of eyes, if not all of them, look at me as I enter. Immediately, I'm the outsider. The one that Rosalind doesn't like. They all know it. It's in their looks and in their frowns.

Lifting my nose up, I stare straight ahead and march over to the table with the food laid out on it. I make my way down the line, filling my plate, then turn at the end. No one is paying attention to me now, which is fine, but I also don't see any of my group here to sit with.

Great. Sitting alone isn't what I really want, but it is what it is. I'll be damned if I'm going to kowtow to Rosalind and her agendas so I can have someone to sit with at dinner. I pick an empty table and sit down, focusing on my food.

Maybe it's paranoia, but maybe it's not. It feels like everyone is looking at me. I don't bother trying to figure it out, so I put all my attention on my plate. I'm too tired to care. I'm almost done when a tiny pair of hands appear in my line of sight, resting on the table.

I look up, and the most adorable Zmaj-human baby, maybe four years old, is sitting across from me. It's shirtless, indicating it's a him, with a shock of hair standing straight up from his head. His horns curl up and back, but his eyes are what grab my attention. Deep intelligence shines in them. He looks more knowing than a child has any right to appear. I've heard of people with 'old souls,' and that best describes him.

He watches me with great interest. When I look up, he doesn't smile or react. He's simply waiting.

"Can I help you?" I ask.

"Hi," he says, his wings briefly fluttering. "I'm Malcolm."

"Hi Malcolm," I say. "I'm An—"

"Annabel, I know," he says.

Okay, then.

"Did you need something?" I ask, looking around for the child's parent. No one is paying any attention to us though.

"No. You do, though," he says.

"I do?"

"Yes," he agrees, nodding sagely. "It's hard though, isn't it?"

"What's hard?" I ask.

"Letting go of the past," he says.

My mind reels and I drop my fork. It clatters to my plate.

"I don't know what you're talking about," I say. "Is your mother near?"

"You do, and she's busy," he says. "She'll be here soon." He smiles. "It's okay. You're going to be important. All of us are. Tajss needs us."

"What do you mean?" I ask.

When he smiles this time, it makes his face have a cherubic look, his full cheeks puffing out, his eyes alight with delight.

"Sometimes you have to act on faith," he says. "Even if it doesn't make sense."

"Malcolm!" A red-headed woman comes into the mess hall and makes a beeline for the two of us.

She grabs the boy up into her arms, and he swings into her, wrapping his arms around her neck.

"Hi, mommy," he says.

"You're supposed to be with Addison," the woman says, then turns to look at me. "Hi, I'm Amara."

She offers a hand that I take, but Malcolm has most of my attention.

"I got bored," Malcolm says. "She's busy in the lab. Ladon's idea is dumb."

"Malcolm!" Amara exclaims. "Watch that mouth."

Malcolm shrugs, unabashed, but doesn't say any more about it.

"What is Ladon's idea?" I ask, curious as to what the boy knows.

"They're trying to deal with the Invaders," Amara explains, overriding Malcolm speaking. "You're Annabel, right?"

"Yes," I say, my stomach clenching tight.

"Cool," she says. "Rosalind wanted to see you. Supposed to tell you if I ran into you."

"Thanks," I say through gritted teeth.

Amara tilts her head to one side and blinks.

"Everything okay?" she asks.

"Sure," I say. "Peachy, even."

"Okay," she says at the same time that Malcolm squirms in her arms. She loses her grip on him and he slides down to the ground, wandering off, and pulling her attention with him. "Kids. I've got to go."

"No problem," I say.

She takes off after the strange boy. How did he know what he did? Was he guessing? How can a boy of no more than a handful of years be wise?

He's right, though. The problem is letting go of the past. How do I let it go? Did I love Quintin? Yes. Yes, I did.

Was it *true love*?

I snort as an old vid that Quintin loved comes to mind. *Wove, Twue Wove.* I don't remember the name of the vid, but Quintin would watch that stick over and over. He could quote every single line of it and did while he watched. It used to drive me nuts. I hated it so much because I was sick of it. I'd seen the vid, why would I watch it again? It's not like the ending changed.

So was what we had true love?

No, I don't think so. Maybe that's it, though. Are there degrees of love? I mean, I love my friends, but they're not my soul mates. I loved my parents, but that's a whole different kind of love, too. Is the answer really that simple? If it is, then am I the soul mate that Calaun spoke of? Is he mine?

The entire idea seems ridiculous yet… right. Something about it feels, I don't know, fitting. Would it be so bad if I did find love? Would I be betraying Quintin?

Sure, he said he wanted me to find someone else if anything happened to him, but everyone says that. Did he mean it? When he said it, the idea of anything happening to either of us was unreal. I didn't take it seriously. The health-care on the ship was top-notch. People didn't die before their natural time. A few, random accidents, but it was so rare that I never knew anyone who did.

A lot different than life on Tajss. Here you can die any minute. Even sitting here at the mess hall there's nothing saying I couldn't be killed between heart beats. There's a cheery thought. I guess I could go full-on depressed about it, but that's never been me.

I pick up my plate, carry it to the collection station, and put it away. Rosalind wants to see me. My heart flutters rapidly and my mouth dries. I've been waiting for this confrontation. I knew it was going to happen, sooner or later. Better later in my opinion, but later has come.

As I drop the plate in the bin, I see my filthy hands. I could clean up. I probably should, but she's the one who put me on this crap detail, so let her see the results. Let her see that I'm not backing down, and I'm sure not afraid to do a hard day's labor. Unlike her in her perfect, always clean, always pristinely white space leathers. Show off.

Decision made, I walk out of the mess hall and across the open courtyard. The fountain makes a soft tinkling sound as the water falls, well, dribbles is more accurate, out of the tip of the statue's lochaber. A handful of people have gathered around the base, sitting on the edge and visiting. They stare as I walk past, but I ignore them, holding my head high.

I'm a working woman. A woman who does what needs doing, and not from some high watch-tower where I overlook all those beneath me. You won't find me spending my time in a hidden office. I'm in the thick of it. Let them look on me and see the truth. I'm a better woman than Rosalind ever will be.

I climb the stairs, and I'm about halfway to her office when I hear another set of footsteps behind me. I keep climbing, cursing every step that's clearly not designed with the shorter human legs in mind. It's exhausting work, and my muscles are burning badly. The footsteps are growing closer, and I've no doubt they'll overtake me in a moment.

"Annabel!" Calaun exclaims.

I stop and lean against the wall as he comes up next to me. I'm out of breath so I can't give a proper greeting back, but I don't miss the weight lifting off my chest or the way my heartbeat seems to be even a bit faster still.

"Hi," I pant.

"Are you okay?" he asks.

"Fine," I gasp, struggling to catch my breath. "Steps are difficult. Too big."

"Ah," he says, staring at the steps and frowning. "I'd not considered it. Let me help you."

He holds his hands out inviting to carry me, but I shake my head. I'm not going to let her win. I've no doubt she chose this office with this stupid climb in mind. She wants those coming to see her to be hot, sweaty, and out of breath before they arrive. He drops his hands to his sides while he waits. I catch my breath and my heart slows down.

"Sorry," I say. "I'm in worse shape than I thought."

"Your *shape* is perfect," he says, his eyes drifting across me.

My cheeks are red hot in an instant, and that pattering heart is right behind them. Why does he have to say things like that? Worse, why do I like it!

"What are you doing here?" I ask, changing the subject away from me.

"One last meeting before I have to go report," he says.

"Oh," I say.

I can't keep the disappointment out of my voice. The look on his face makes it clear he heard it too. Damn it. I shouldn't be disappointed. he's not mine. I'm not his. Despite his romanticizing of our one-night stand. Or so I'm going to keep telling myself, as I try to avoid a truth I'm not ready for, at least not yet.

I'm closer.

"Shall we continue?" he asks, offering an arm.

I take it before I can think about it too much, and together we resume climbing the stairs. He's obviously slowing his pace down to match my much slower one. It's fine, though. I'm not going to debate the fact I'm enjoying time with him. When I look down at my arm wrapped around his and see my hand resting on his forearm, I gasp, pull my arm free, and step back.

"What is it?" he asks.

"I'm a mess," I say, shaking my head.

"You've put in a full day's work," he says. "This is admirable."

"And I haven't washed since," I say, holding my hands up.

They're almost black with filth. I'm disgusting. Going to see Rosalind it seemed like a good idea, but I hadn't considered running into Calaun. Now I'm embarrassed. He smiles and shakes his head.

"I do not mind," he says.

"Sure, you say that now," I say. "But look at me. I've got layers of dirt caked onto the layers of dirt."

"And yet your beauty is undiminished," he says.

"Your impossible," I say, but when he says things like that, it warms my skin and my lady-parts.

He's sincere and there's no denying it. He really thinks I'm the most beautiful woman. There's something wonderful about it.

"Yes," he agrees. "I probably am. I'm not going to pretend. I don't understand how I could be so lucky as to have two females. Maybe it wasn't. Maybe it's not but I know what I feel. And I know what I see."

I smile and a tear wells in my eye. I want to wipe it away, but I don't want to get dirt in my eyes. I don't know why I'm crying, but he's moving me. I'm broken down and bare in front of him. I've got nothing to offer him, yet he accepts me as I am. Bitchy, dirty, lost and holding on to the past, but he takes me as I am.

What more could I ask of any man? We keep climbing and I fight with the lump in my throat. I can't deal with the storm of emotions that he's creating in me, so I focus on the next step.

Rosalind is going to be at the end of these steps. I don't know why she wants to see me. Probably to lord it over me. Rub my face in how far I've fallen. I had freedom. A kingdom. Small, sure, but it was mine. Now I've lost it all to her.

She didn't even have to do anything. It was her good luck and my bad that switched our positions. If I'd crashed with the main group of survivors like she did, then I'd probably be in a leadership position, not her. I'd be better at it too. Kinder. I'd never let myself lord it over everyone else, holding myself apart as if I'm too good for them. Look at me, the dirt caked on to me proves that!

Focusing on Rosalind helps. The anger is warm and familiar, and I know what to do with anger. All these other feelings and emotions that Calaun has awakened, that's confusion. I don't need confusion. Anger will serve much better.

He pushes the door open at the top of the stairs and holds it for me. When I step through, I brush against the hard muscles of his chest and stomach. My skin fevers at even this brushing contact. Memories of him over me, thrusting in, burst to the forefront of my thoughts. It distracts me, and I trip over something as I step forward.

As I stumble ahead, struggling to keep my balance, he catches me by my waist and puts me back onto my feet. He doesn't let go. Strong hands, fingers curling around my hips and resting on my stomach.

I straighten and slowly, reluctantly, I step out of his hands. His fingers linger, touching as long as they can as I move ahead. I don't want to take the next step. It's stupid, but this simple touch awakens a throbbing desire. A need to be held. To know I'm cared for, and it's not all on me. The tears well back into my eyes, but I blink them away.

I'm about to face Rosalind. I don't have time to handle him or my emotions. It's time to set the record straight on what my life here in the City is going to be. I'm not going to be her whipping post.

Squaring my shoulders, I glance at him, giving him a smile. None of this has anything to do with him, it's about her. I'm not going to hurt his feelings because he happens to be here at the wrong moment.

"Thank you," I say.

"Of course," he says, slowly lowering his hands to his sides.

"You want to deal with her first?" I ask.

"How about we go together?" he asks.

I frown, unsure I want him there when I face off with my nemesis. On one hand I'd love his support in there with me. On the other hand, I don't want him there if I lose. What am I thinking? I'm not going to lose.

"Sure," I agree, making my decision.

We walk to the double doors side by side, close but not too close. No touching. Can't get distracted when I'm in it to win it. The doors swing open under our hands and we walk through.

There she is. My enemy. The Queen in white. My shoulders knot the instant I see her and my head aches. I clench my jaw, straighten my back, and march across the room to meet her. She smiles, rising to her feet and walking to meet me.

She's immaculately clean, her hair is perfect, and no one has skin that flawless. She must be wearing makeup. An extravagance if I ever saw one. She extends a hand, and I look at it for a pointed moment before extending my own to take it.

"Annabel," she says, giving no attention to my current filthy state. "I'm so glad you've come to the City."

"Of course," I answer.

"Calaun, I thought you'd be on your way back to the Order by now," she says, letting my hand go and turning her attention to him.

"Soon," he says. "I wanted to discuss this plan with you first."

"I see," she says, her eyes moving between the two of us.

I'm sure she's heard rumors at the very least of his interest in me. He hasn't been secretive about his interest in me and I'm sure she has spies everywhere.

"I was told you wanted to see me," I interrupt the moment.

"Yes," she says, motioning towards seats at the table.

The table. Where the high and mighty 'council' meets. Biting my tongue, I take the offered seat. She's up to something, and now I have to play along to find out what.

"Would either of you like some water?" she asks, standing behind her seat.

"No, thank you," I say.

Calaun also declines the offer, and Rosalind takes a seat.

"As I was saying, I'm glad you've all decided to come to the City, Annabel," Rosalind says. "I didn't like your group being out there alone."

"We were doing fine," I say.

"Of course you were," she smiles, but it doesn't touch her eyes. "You're a strong, independent woman. A leader."

She doesn't say more, watching me, silent. The moment becomes awkward, and I'm fighting the urge to squirm in my seat under her watchful gaze.

"Thanks," I say at last.

Rosalind smiles and nods. "You've earned it. You know, I believe, what my post was on the ship?"

"Of course," I say.

"I was the Lady General, in charge of all the armed forces of the ship."

"Yeah," I say, biting off my urge to ask how that worked out since we got invaded and crashed.

"The one thing I learned in that position is to recognize talent," she says. "The Armed Forces work on structure and leadership. You have to see the leaders in your group, groom them, and put them in charge."

She stares again, silently waiting, for what I don't know. I'm trying not to give into it again. If I don't answer her, maybe she'll speak her piece, and I can get to a shower and bed. I'm too tired for this verbal sparring. I wait and wait, but she doesn't continue. Even Calaun shifts in his seat.

"Is there a point to this?" I snap at last.

"Direct," she says. "I like that. Yes, there is. I want to offer you a seat on the Council."

"You—" I say, but I've got nothing more than that single syllable.

I shut my mouth and let my thoughts coalesce into something resembling a whole. Calaun is grinning and looking over at me, while Rosalind watches every aspect of how I take this offer. What is her game? Why a seat at the table? Why me?

Keep your enemies close? Is that the game? Studying her face, I try to find any tell, some sign of what her true intentions are, but I can't find a hint of anything but sincerity.

"Why?" I blurt out, unable to figure it out for myself, but I'm not going to accept anything from her on a charity basis.

"I believe I've told you the why," she says. "But to clarify, I like your style. You've kept your group safe in the desert, with the help of a single, elder Zmaj, sure, but they follow you. They're loyal to you, and you care about them.

"These are trying times, and they're not going to get easier. We have to be united. I'm handling a bigger picture than most of the survivors realize, but at the same time, I need capable people who can handle the day-to-day activities. Leaders who care, who will make sure that our people are taken care of in the short-term, not only the long-term."

Calaun takes my hand under the table. His hand holding mine becomes an anchor as my world spins around me. She's sincere. My nemesis, my great enemy has disarmed me without a shot fired. She's admitting her weaknesses and asking me to help her make up for them.

It has to be a lie. This isn't the demon woman that I was prepared to face. This isn't the uncaring overlord dominating the world for her personal pleasure. I'm spinning. My mouth is dry and butterflies dance in my stomach.

"Is this a joke?" I ask.

She frowns and her forehead wrinkles, marring her perfect façade. Now I see the crow's feet at the corners of her eyes, the gray at her temples. Stress lines. Have I judged her wrong? Is she not the monster I perceived?

"Why would you think that?" she asks.

I bite my lip, debating, how do I answer that? The truth is too complicated, it's not a simple answer at all.

"I've learned," I say at last. "To not trust easily."

Rosalind nods. Calaun squeezes my hand but doesn't intervene. I glance at him out of the corner of my eye and see his respect. He's letting me fight my battle, supporting me, but not doing it for me.

"I see," she says, leaning onto the table. "I'm sure it's been rough, being out there on your own. Those girls depending on you. I can only imagine how hard it was. There were a lot of advantages we had with finding the City and a better set of supplies."

"Sure," I agree. "But that doesn't answer the question. Is this a joke?"

"No," she says, and there is a weariness in her voice and manner that comes through. "It's not. Annabel, we're dancing on the verge of extinction. The Zmaj had consigned themselves to it, and after we lost the ship..." she trails off. Her jaw tenses, hands close to fists and she looks up, meeting my eyes for the first time since she started speaking. "Since I lost the ship."

Her pain is so clear in her simple statement, in that single admission of her guilt, that my heart breaks for her. I feel her regret, and it lies heavy on the room now that she's put it out there. She's opened herself up, laid herself bare before me.

This is my moment. Do I accept her admission of guilt?

Was this rivalry really only in my head? She stares at the table, and I stare at her. We wait, for what I don't know. It seems the ball is in my court, but this isn't the way I ever imagined a victory over my rival.

A victory should come along with fanfare, some glory, not this ignoble end for her and the rivalry I've nursed for so long. Calaun runs his hand up and down my forearm. I look at him and he nods, encouraging me.

"Thank you," I say at long last.

"For what?" Rosalind asks, looking up.

"For admitting it," I say. "You should have saved us. It was your duty. None of this should have happened."

"You're right," she sighs. "We were betrayed, but that doesn't absolve me. I didn't see it coming. There were warnings, but I didn't act fast enough."

There's a lot in what she says that I'd like to know more about, but I'm exhausted. This isn't the time. I always promised myself I wouldn't be lording it over anyone if I was a leader. That's not me, and I'm not going to become that person. As such, the only thing I can do is move forward and let her move forward too.

"We can't change the past," I say, and immediately regret is sour in my mouth.

Quintin, I have so many regrets regarding him. Regrets that bind me to the past. Every day has been surviving the moment. Getting through what is happening, but when was the last time I looked ahead?

"No, we can't," she agrees. "We can create a future. A better future, for all of us. Human and Zmaj both."

"This is a good thing," Calaun says. "This is the way forward."

I look over to him, and my heart races, breath coming short. His eyes are on me, intense and filled with promises of a future if only I'll open my heart. I can't hold onto the past but staring into an uncertain future fills me with gut-clenching fear. A lump forms in my throat. I swallow hard, forcing it down and nod.

"Okay," I agree, except I'm not only agreeing to Rosalind, I'm agreeing to Calaun.

I'm agreeing that there can be a future. That we could, together, create something more than living in this singular moment. Something more than surviving.

"Good," Rosalind says. "So there are things I've not let be broadly distributed. Information that is restricted to members of the Council only. I'll need your agreement and understanding that this is not be to be spoken of in public. I don't want to cause panic and fear."

"What kind of things?" I ask.

"Your agreement must come first," she says. "I will consider your oath binding."

"And how do you know I will keep my word?" I counter.

Rosalind smiles but it's a cold, heartless smile that doesn't touch her eyes. "I can smell bullshit a mile away."

She's serious and I believe her.

"Okay, I give my word to keep the confidences I hear or learn in Council."

"Good," she says. "Calaun, our agreements with the Order remain in full force. You will not share this information with anyone but your own leaders."

"Of course," he agrees and Rosalind nods.

"The Invaders are coming from off-planet," Rosalind says. "That's first and probably not a surprise. What you don't know is that Tajss was at the center of a Galactic Civil War. One waged to control it, that war led to the event known as the Devastation."

"I'm not surprised," I say, "but I didn't know it for sure."

"Smart," Rosalind says. "There is a plan forming to counterattack the Invaders."

I nod and keep my mouth shut, carefully not looking at Calaun so as not to betray that he already told me this.

"What is it?" I ask.

"It's in the works," she says vaguely. "That's the first bit of business you'll learn about as a Council Member. It's important you be briefed on this but it's only part of the problems we're dealing with."

"Great, there's more?" I ask.

"Yes," Rosalind says. "Our population. It's my primary concern and why we can't afford to lose anyone. Have you heard the term, minimum viable population?"

"No," I say.

"In layman's terms it means the minimum number of different, non-related persons required for a group to be viable," she says.

"What do you mean 'viable'," I ask.

"If we drop below that minimum number the odds of there not being cross-contamination of lines of DNA become statistically impossible. We would literally breed ourselves out of existence."

That leaves a cold, harsh taste in my mouth. The way she says it is clinical, detached. As if it's not human lives she's talking about but any regular commodity.

"How close are we to dropping below this minimum?" I ask.

"Too close," Rosalind says. "The Invaders are making it worse. We can't afford to lose anyone, yet these attacks keep happening. So far, they haven't attacked with lethal force. Their intent seems to be on capture, not killing."

"But you're concerned if this goes on too long, they'll change their tactic," I say.

"Yes," Rosalind agrees.

Calaun pats my leg under the table. He's smiling from ear to ear, but doesn't speak.

"So what do we do about it?" I ask.

"This is why we're exploring counter-attacks," Rosalind says. "We have to stop the attacks, but more than that we have to keep them from letting any others in the broader galaxy out there know that Tajss is alive."

"So what is it they want here? I can't imagine slavery is viable, there's not enough people here to make that worth it, are there?" I ask

"I don't think so," Rosalind says.

"We thought at first they were here to collect the meteorite glass," Calaun says. "As you can imagine, it would be infinitely easier to collect it from a planet that had passed through the field than to set up a mining operation in space for it."

"Makes senses, but there hasn't been fresh glass in quite a while," I say.

"Exactly," Rosalind says.

Then what are they looking for? I think it over, then it hits me.

"Epis," I say, and Rosalind nods.

"If they're here for epis, then the problem will grow," Rosalind says. "We need to stop them from getting epis, and getting off-planet."

"The planet is huge, why don't they go anywhere besides where we are and gather it up?" I ask.

"That's an insightful question," Rosalind says.

My cheeks warm at the compliment, and it hits me that she's truly not my enemy. I'd thought it but not really let it sink in. Here I am, sitting and discussing strategy with her. She invited me to a seat at her table. I shake my head in disbelief. This is the most unreal thing that's happened to me since, well since Calaun declared his love. Calaun gives me a reassuring grip of the leg, but still, he remains silent.

"What is it you need of me?" I ask. It's the obvious question.

"Insight," she says, "first and foremost. Also I need someone who can keep in touch with the people. It's impossible for me to keep my finger on the pulse. On what they need as compared to what the whole needs. I need someone who can bring that perspective to the table. It's something our Council is sorely lacking."

"Agreed," I say without hesitation.

"Good," she nods. "Now, Calaun, what is it you wished to discuss with me?"

"I would like to join the team going to find the old space port," he says.

"I'm surprised you don't already know where it is," Rosalind says.

Calaun's tail goes stock still but the smile remains fixed on his face. "Why would you think such a thing?"

"Why, indeed?" she asks, pursing her lips. "The Order most often seems to know most things well before I do."

"The Order has our mission," he says.

"Which is what, again?" she asks.

Calaun smiles. "So am I to take this as a no?"

"I'm considering it," Rosalind says.

"I'd like to go too," I offer.

Only the subtlest widening of her eyes shows her surprise. "Why would you go?"

"I'm interested," I say. "If I'm going to integrate into the City and be seen as someone they can trust, I need to be seen to pull my weight. Doing grunt work isn't going to be enough."

I'm making this up on the fly. The only reason I volunteered for this was an impulse. A stupid desire to not let Calaun go, at least not yet. If he goes back to the Order, how do I know I'll ever see him again?

"Fine," Rosalind says.

Exhaustion hits me hard, so I rise to my feet. I'd been dreading this, and now that it all went better than I could have ever imagined, all I want is a fast bath and a bed.

"Is there anything else?" I ask.

"No, that's all," Rosalind says. "Welcome to Draconov."

"Thank you," I say, turning and walking out the door.

I keep my back straight and my knees from wobbling until I'm on the far side of the door, but that's as far as I can hold it together. Once those doors close, I'm shaky as a leaf on the wind. I make my way to one of the waiting area chairs and plop down.

"Are you okay?" Calaun asks.

"Fine," I say, waving one hand weakly. "It's nothing."

"This does not look like nothing," he says. "Should I get help?"

"No!" I say, forcing myself to sit up straight. "I'm fine. Seriously."

He studies me with an intensity that warms my chest. Damn, why does he have this effect on me? This would be easier if I was alone. He takes a seat next to me.

"Annabel," he says, softly. "I want to help."

There it is again, that resonating sincerity that he always speaks with. Damn if it's not frustrating. Every time he does it, my heart melts.

"Calaun," I say, placing my hand on his. "It's nothing, it was stupid. I had thought that Rosalind was a rival. That she and I were against each other, yet here I am now being offered a seat on the Council. Everything I believed, all the reasons I stayed away from the City, were a lie. It's a lot to take in, that's all."

"Oh," he says, falling silent.

We sit in a silence that is entirely too comfortable and too easy for people who barely know each other. And then there's that. That is even more intimidating. I've got to let Quintin go. I know, all things as they are, he wouldn't want me to not live, and I'm not.

I've been hiding. Literally hiding to a large degree in the desert. Avoiding the City because of a rivalry that for all appearances only existed in my head. Because it was a good way to avoid the truth. I couldn't let go. I didn't want to.

Now a future has almost literally knocked down the door, and all I have to do is say yes. Take his hand in mine and... what?

Live.

I have to live.

"Calaun," I say. "Yes."

"Yes?" he asks.

The butterflies in my stomach feel like they're trying to climb out of my throat. I swallow hard, but a cold sweat has formed across my arms and back. I blink rapidly as my nerves get the better of me. I want to say more, but my mouth feels as dry as the sands outside the dome. Struggling I finally get the words to come out.

"I want to... know. I want to try," I say. "Us. I want to try us."

"Are you sure?" he asks.

"No," I admit. His warm eyes bore into mine pulling the truth. "I'm terrified."

He touches my face with the tips of his fingers and trails them along my jaw. His touch is cool but my skin fevers at it anyway.

"It is okay to be afraid," he says. "Natural, even."

"You're not," I counter.

"Aren't I?" he asks. He shakes his head. "I may hide it well, but I will never lie to you. I am afraid. Though I ask myself, what is fear? For me, it's the unknown. I know what I feel for you, but it contradicts what I've believed my entire life. That Zmaj's mate once, for life."

"That's scary, too," I admit. "For me. What if all you're feeling for me is a chemical imbalance in your brain?"

"No, there is no mistaking this," he says. "The dragon has chosen. Now the journey is to find the truth of why and how."

"We humans don't have it that easy," I say.

"I understand," he says. "We'll take it slow. We can… what is the term you humans use? Date?"

I laugh. "Date, yes."

"Good, then we shall date."

"Okay," I agree. "No commitment, not yet."

"You will see," he says. "I am sure of it."

I pat his hand and smile.

"I hope so," I say. "For now, I need a bath."

13

ANNABEL

I wake with a start, cold sweat drying on my skin. Dimly remembered dreams fading as soon as I open my eyes. I don't recall what they were, but my heart pounds and that lingering feeling of fear retreats its icy touch slowly.

I walk over to the small cleaning station and splash room temperature water on my face then run my fingers through my hair, fixing it the best I can. Once I've done that I dress and head for the door. I'm supposed to meet Calaun and Ladon for the trip outside today.

An adventure, yay.

I guess I should be excited, but I'm not. I can't shake this feeling that something is going to go wrong today. Horribly wrong but I've got no idea what it is I'm worried about. I'll be with two Zmaj males. It's about as safe as you can get if you live on this planet.

When I open the door something moves from the shadows outside and I yelp trying to shut the door fast. It slams against a stop and there's a grunt.

"Annabel," Calaun says.

"What are you doing?" I ask, doing my best to not screech.

My heart is in my throat, and my stomach is a tight knot.

"Waiting for you," he says. "I did not wish to disturb your rest but wanted to be here when you woke."

It's the sweetest and stupidest thing I've ever heard. Both at once which is quite an accomplishment, really. Is this what a relationship with him is going to be like? I'd better lay down some ground rules right now.

"Okay, look," I say. "This is too much."

"What is?" he asks.

"You've got to give me some space," I say.

"I did," he agrees. "I watched outside your door."

"For how long?" I ask.

He has the grace to look sheepish. "All night."

"Are you kidding me?" I ask.

"No?" he makes it a question, but I know he's serious.

I roll my eyes and shake my head.

"Start with that," I say. "That's not giving me space. That's being… too much. We're barely dating, okay? This isn't instant love or whatever. This is two people figuring out if they're compatible, got it?"

"Compatible?" he asks. "I don't understand. We've already established our bodies are compatible."

My cheeks burn red hot and I take a step back sputtering.

"That is *not* what I meant by that!"

"Oh," he says, shaking his head. "Then I do not understand."

"Oh my god," I exhale struggling to get my emotions under control. "Look, dating. I told you about this, it's getting to know one another. I want to know you, see if I really like you or if it's just an itch."

"An itch?" he asks.

I glare, and he steps back into the hall. "Perhaps we should be moving? Ladon will be waiting."

"Good idea," I say, pushing my way past.

I lead the way out of the building my rooms are in and towards the fountain, which is the central locale for the City. Ladon is waiting when we approach.

"Good morning," Ladon says.

"Morning," I answer. "We should go."

"I agree," Ladon says. "The suns are already high."

I don't have a glare left for Ladon, and besides, he's right. I was already late waking up and then taking time to debate with Calaun cost even more time. Ladon leads the way, and it isn't long before we're stepping free of the dome and out into the open desert air.

The heat of it is impressively oppressive. I haven't been in the City that long, yet here I am acclimating to the cooler air already. The heat out here takes my breath away for a moment while my lungs adjust to the temperature.

"This way," Ladon says, heading for a dune to the southwest.

Calaun and I follow along behind him. I pride myself on how little help I need from Calaun as we work our way across the loose sands. There's a trick to how you put your weight down that keeps you from sinking in too deep.

It's too hot for small talk, but we make what seems to be good time. Ladon doesn't seem to agree, not that he says anything out loud. He does keep looking back with a deep frown. The suns are high in the sky, about midday I'd guess, when Ladon stops.

"This is the area," he says.

We're standing on top of a massive dune, high enough that it gives a decent view of the surrounding area. I turn in a slow circle, shielding my eyes with a hand. There's nothing in sight except more sand. Rolling dune after rolling dune. Calaun stands beside me but he's watching me. Ladon sets down his pack and digs into it.

"This doesn't look very hopeful," I say, trying to not be mean.

Ladon looks over his shoulder. "It was here."

"Okay," I say, shaking my head and looking at Calaun for his input.

Calaun looks around then kneels and pushes his hand into the sand.

"It could be," he says.

Ladon pulls out a shovel that he tosses to Calaun then gets out another for himself. The two men start digging. It's hard work since the sand wants to pour back in as fast as they dig it out. I make myself useful by pulling the piles further out using my hands since there are no other tools.

It's back-breaking work. We're at it for a long time and a sizable hole is being created, when Ladon drives his shovel down and it hits something solid. The two men share a look, then go to work even faster. Sand flies out of the hole which is probably four feet deep now. I move as fast as I can to keep the sand moving out of the way.

It isn't long before we can see there's metal. They start digging to either side but all they find is more metal. No signs of an opening or a way we can get through the metal.

"This is impossible," I say at last.

"There is no way to tell where the entrance might have been," Calaun says.

"We have to find a way in," Ladon says.

Suddenly he takes the shovel in both hands and slams it against the metal with incredible force. The blade of the shovel bends, the metal plate clangs, but he doesn't stop. He rains down blow after blow against the metal. Puffs of sand burst into the air around him with each blow, and then I hear a hiss of escaping gas. Ladon roars. Rising to his feet, he drives the bent blade against the metal over and over. His muscles bulge, his face contorts, his rage boils over.

It's terrifying. I scramble back from the opening as his blows get wilder. Calaun leaps out of the hole, his wings spreading, and he lands between Ladon and me. Ladon continues until the metal part of the shovel breaks off, and he's left holding a broken haft.

He throws his arms into the air and screams, shaking the broken stick at the sky above. He drops to his knees and pounds the metal with his fists. Calaun jumps back into the hole and grabs Ladon.

Ladon fights to continue pounding the metal, but Calaun wrestles him. The two men fight back and forth. Ladon lands a harsh blow to Calaun's jaw. It hits with a crunch that makes me sick to my stomach.

Ladon throws himself backwards into Calaun taking advantage of the opening. They crash to the sand with Ladon on top. He slams his elbows into Calaun over and over. The smacking of flesh onto flesh hurts my ears and tears at my heart.

He's going to kill Calaun. I can't let him do this. I don't know what's happening or why Ladon has suddenly gone crazy, but I'm not going to stand by and let this happen. Even if I wasn't interested in Calaun, I can't stand here doing nothing.

The fighting continues as I look for something, anything I can do to help. I'm not stupid. Obviously, something is happening to Ladon, and there is no way I can take him out or probably hurt him without a tool.

My eyes land on the haft of the shovel. It's about three feet of solid-looking wood broken off into a jagged end. It's the only thing that I can use, except it's close to where the two men are fighting.

They're rolling over and over, struggling to gain the advantage of being on top. Ladon is growling. A deep, rumbling sound that's completely primal. Calaun is yelling at him to control himself, but Ladon is acting like an animal.

The choice is clear, so I run for the handle. My feet sink into the sand slowing me down, but I move as fast as I can. More blows land, but I'm not taking time to see who is hitting whom. I've got tunnel vision on the handle.

I'm almost to it when a particularly vicious crack echoes through my ears. I glance in their direction and Ladon has Calaun in a choke hold. Calaun is gripping Ladon's arm, but the color of his face is changing.

Heart racing, I leap forward, stretching my arm out as far as I can. I land face first in the sand, but my fingertips brush the handle. Crawling forward is easier than walking in the loose sand. I make my way ahead until I get a good grip on the handle.

On my knees I look at the two men. The chokehold is still in place, and it's clear that Calaun is growing weaker. He's fighting less, and his eyes are drifting closed.

Adrenaline pumps into my body. That's my man! I'm not going to lose him when I only considered the possibility of having him. We haven't had enough time!

Stumbling through the sand, I run the best I can. It's slow. Too slow. Calaun punches with one hand, hitting Ladon in the face, but it doesn't faze Ladon. The blow is too weak.

Calaun changes tactic, fighting to get a grip on Ladon's arm. He slams his tail into Ladon at the same time he kicks at his leg. Ladon falls backwards but he pulls Calaun down with him.

Calaun jerks and thrusts. Ladon is under him, pulling down tight with his chokehold. Calaun twists from side to side and the two of them roll, but now Ladon is on top. Ladon pulls back, rising up.

He doesn't see me coming. I'm right behind him. I grip

the wooden handle tight in both hands, raising it over my head. Calaun makes a gurgling sound.

I swing the handle with everything I've got. It cracks loudly when it hits Ladon's head. Ladon falls to the side in a heap, and I drop to my knees next to Calaun.

Calaun gasps. He sits up and looks around wildly. His eyes land on me, and then he shifts in an instant, putting himself between me and Ladon's now prone form. He thrusts an arm protectively back and moves backwards, forcing me along behind him.

His breath is raspy and ragged as he focuses on breathing. Only when we've got some distance between us and Ladon does he stop and glance over his shoulder.

"Are you okay?" he asks.

My tears fall unrestrained. He was literally choked out, and his first question is if I'm okay. It hits me that this is my man. The way my heart races. There's so much pressure on my chest it's hard to breathe. My skin tingles and I want nothing more than to kiss him in this singularly insane moment. We're in immediate danger, and all I want is to have him wrap his arms around me and kiss me like there's no tomorrow.

Is this love?

If this isn't love, then what is?

"I love you!" I blurt out.

Our eyes lock together as the world stops. Cold chills spread across the back of my neck and shoulders. Disbelief that I said it mixes with relief. It's true. I don't know if it's fate, soulmates, or only two people being compatible.

It's more than I care for him. The way he makes me feel is beyond words, but when I'm with him there is certainty. The moment breaks, and he moves, wrapping his arms around me, his lips crushing against mine.

My body melds against his. His hard muscles force my

softness to shape against him. His tongue brushes my lips, his hands roam down my back. I twine my fingers in his hair.

He breaks the kiss, holding me close for a moment longer before he lets me go and turns back to where Ladon lies on the sand.

"I must tend to him," he says.

As he moves away, his touch lingers on mine, and I stretch my arm to keep that contact with him as long as possible. It's selfish, and I know it, but at least I can admit it.

Calaun kneels next to Ladon, placing a hand on his neck. He frowns then moves his hand to Ladon's forehead and cheeks.

"He's burning up," he says.

I go to him and feel for myself. Ladon is warm, not overly warm if he was a human, considering we're in the desert under two red suns, but for a Zmaj, he's boiling. The Zmaj are closer to what earth biology would consider cold-blooded, part of why they're better adapted to life here on Tajss.

"What do we do?" I ask.

"Get him back to the City," Calaun says.

He grabs Ladon's arm and lifts him up. In moments he has him slung over his shoulders, and we make our overly slow way back to the City.

14

CALAUN

Ladon's weight makes the return trip to the City harder. The suns are below the horizon when we approach the airlock.

He has a fever, which is not something a Zmaj normally displays. It's against our biological nature for us to ever have one, and I'm only aware of the idea because I've studied the human physiology.

Combine this fever with how he attacked first the metal we uncovered then me, and there is something seriously wrong. I don't know what, but it's not good. The guard at the airlock is sleepy and barely alert when we come through.

"We need medical attention," I order.

"What?" the guard asks.

"Ladon is sick, we need medical!" Annabel yells at him.

"Oh, well, no need to yell," the man says.

Annabel opens her mouth to retort, so I put a hand on her shoulder. She whips her head in my direction, eyes afire with rage, but I shake my head.

"Please get the medical staff alerted," I say. "I'm taking him to the facility."

"Sure," the man says, shaking his head and yawning.

"Now," I say. "Please."

The man rolls his eyes and then wanders off into the City, leaving his post abandoned. I push down my own anger because there is no time for it. Attitudes and activities like this would never be tolerated in the Order. That man would be whipped, which would make sure he knew better next time.

"Come on," Annabel says. "I know the way."

I follow her through the City. Watching her lead, the memory of what happened between us replays in my mind. She said the words. Did she mean them? I've replayed it in my mind over and over as we raced across the desert as fast as we could. She said she loved me. I want to ask. I want, desperately, to hear her say it again, but now is not the time.

We round a corner and see Sverre running to us.

"What happened?" he asks, seeing Ladon over my shoulders.

"He went crazy," Annabel answers.

"I had to subdue him," I add.

"Why?" Sverre asks.

"I don't know," I say. "We dug through the sand, found metal that we couldn't get through, and then it was like his bijass took over completely."

"Get him inside, I'll make sure help arrives," Sverre says, running away as he talks.

We enter the medical facility, and I put Ladon down on one of the beds, but no one else is here. There are machines all over the place, but my medical training is in no way up to this task. I know basic treatments, mostly for battle wounds to be dressed in the field.

"He needs help," I say.

When I feel his face, I can tell he's hotter now than he was. The temperature is spiking. I grab my water skin where

I left it lying on the floor and hold the tip of it to his mouth. Water pours into his mouth, then out and across his face. He swallows some but I don't want to drown him, so I stop.

"I don't know how to find anyone," Annabel says.

"I will try," I say. "Stay with him, please."

She nods and moves to the bedside. I touch her shoulder before I walk to the door. I stop and look back, suddenly worried. I don't want to leave her alone. Ladon was out of his mind out there in the sands. If he wakes up, he might hurt her. I'm stuck in a moment of indecision when the door slams into me.

"Get out of the way!" a female yells from the other side of the door, slamming it into me again.

I move to one side before it swings again.

Crack!

It hits the wall and Annabel jumps. Addison rushes through without a side glance, followed by another Zmaj I don't know.

"Get away from him," she orders Annabel.

"Wha— Why?" Annabel protests.

"He's got a fever?" Addison asks.

"Yes," Annabel says.

"Then get out of here," she barks. She looks at the Zmaj with her. "You too, Ormarr."

Ormarr stops, turns and walks out of the room. Annabel opens her mouth to protest, but when she sees Ormarr leaving without an argument, she follows him. I bring up the rear and let the door close behind me.

"What is going on?" Annabel asks Ormarr.

"We don't know," he says.

"What does that mean?" Annabel asks.

"Zmaj do not get 'fevers,'" I answer, putting the pieces together.

Annabel snaps her mouth shut. Her brow furrows in the

most delightful way as she purses her lips and thinks. It's her 'concentrating' face, and I love it dearly. With every beating of my heart, I know she's the one.

The impossible has come to pass, and what that means, I can't even pretend to know. Everything I've ever believed has changed. Good or bad remains to be seen, but how can love be bad? How can two souls finding each other be wrong?

Except I'd found my mate and lost her. It leads me to the one open question. What happens to the lost soul?

It's not a question I've ever asked. Zmaj mates normally passed together so there was no need to consider the possibility. If one died prematurely, the remaining one waited out their time, then rejoined them in the after. I don't know of it being otherwise. What happens to the one who went early though?

"Fever means contagious," Annabel says at last. "In humans. Is it the same for Zmaj?"

"We don't know," Ormarr replies.

"I need to warn the others," Annabel says.

"No," Ormarr says, moving to block her exit. "You may be carrying whatever this is."

"You're kidding me," Annabel says.

"No," Ormarr says. "I'm not."

"So we're in quarantine?" she asks.

"It would be the wisest move," Ormarr says. "So yes."

"Are you thinking he contracted something out there?" she asks.

"Honestly?" Ormarr asks and Annabel nods. "I hope so."

She frowns, showing her concentrating face again. "Why?"

"Because if he already had the sickness before he left here today—if it *is* a sickness—our problems will be much bigger," Ormarr answers. "I need to check you both out."

"Yeah," Annabel says, taking a seat.

I sit beside her, my thoughts spinning at the implications. This is an unforeseen challenge. I'll need to report to the Order as soon as possible, but I agree that if we are carrying an illness, we can't risk carrying it out to the others in the population.

"Sverre," I say and Ormarr stops his work.

"What about him?" Ormarr asks.

"He saw us, as did the human male who was on duty at the airlock," I say.

Ormarr closes his eyes and clenches his jaw.

"Got it," he says.

"What do we do?" Annabel asks.

"Hope that this isn't contagious," Ormarr says. "Or we have a much bigger problem."

I take Annabel's hand in mine while Ormarr does his work. I know, with absolute certainty, that this will work out. If fate meant our souls to meet, then it cannot be that we would lose each other so soon after finding one another.

That doesn't help everyone else, but for now it's all I've got to cling to while we wait to see.

15

CALAUN

"I didn't mean that we had to be locked away together to have time to get to know each other," Annabel complains, not for the first time.

She paces the room again. I watch her walk, studying her gait, the lines of her body, of her face. Sunlight coming through the window outlines her form. A reddish-golden glow surrounds her body, giving her a fiery look that makes her look like an angel of fire.

Rising to my feet, I step into her path, putting my hands on her waist. She stops and looks up. Worry lines her face, so I do the only thing I can to help. I kiss each line of worry, soft and gentle, until the concern drops from her face and she moans softly.

"You're impossible," she says.

"I might be," I agree. "We are impossible. Yet here we are."

"Yes," she says, wrapping her arms around my neck and molding her body to mine.

Wrapping my arms around her, I hold her tight against me. Our flesh melds together as if it was made for each other. It was. We are meant to be.

"I do like your idea," she whispers in my ear.

"Which?" I ask.

"That we are soulmates," she says. "I don't know… but it does feel like I've known you much longer than I have."

I smile and nod.

"That is a good thing," I say.

"Yeah, I don't mind," she says kissing me with gentle touches of her lips to mine. "It seems impossible, but who knows? It's obviously a very big universe. If we were… if it's true, I mean, the fact that an entire generation ship, millions of lives crashed here for us? That's an overwhelming thought."

"I hadn't considered that," I admit.

"I have," she says. "That's what bothers me about it. All those people losing their lives so I could find my other soul half?"

We hold each other tight as I think about what she's said. It is a dark thought, but somehow it doesn't fit. She's right that it doesn't make sense. Love will find a way, but not at the cost of so many.

"So many Zmaj have found their mates," I say, running my fingers through her hair. She murmurs agreement into my chest.

I want to say more. I want to reveal all my secrets to her, all the deeply held beliefs, the agenda of the Order as I know it. I want to, but I'm sworn to secrecy. My duty, my responsibility to Tajss is above all. Is it above love too?

I don't know.

How can it be? The dragon stirs in my soul, breathing its fire, making my blood pump hot. I'm acutely aware of her body pressing against me. My prime cock stiffens between us and she wiggles, teasing it in response.

She leans her head back, offering me her lips. We've been locked in here for three days. They bring us food and water regularly, but there is no news except they are still caring for Ladon. The days would be monotonous if I didn't have Annabel to help me pass my time.

Her brilliant mind, beautiful body, all of which she has been offering to me freely. Desire is rising, but the questions she has posed ride over the top of it. Duty binds me tightly. I won't reveal the secrets, but how do I hold them back?

When I agreed to keep the secrets of the Order, I did not know what love would feel like. The love I knew before was forgotten in the fog of the past. There was nothing left of it for me to know better than to agree. It's tearing at me not telling her all.

"Annabel," I say at last, taking her by her shoulders and pushing her back so we're looking into each other's eyes. "I want to tell you something."

"That's never a good start to a conversation," she says, her eyes narrowing.

"It is fine," I say. "Take a seat, please."

We sit and I try to find the words to say what I want to say. Though I want to tell her everything, I can't. Some things won't make sense to her, some I can't put into words, some of it is too much to say at once. Right now I want—no, I need—her to understand the ideals of the Order.

"What do you know of the Order?" I ask.

"Not much. Group of Zmaj, fairly secretive," she says. "I've not been in the City, so my understanding is limited."

I nod. "The Order is dedicated to Tajss itself."

"To the planet?" she asks, and I nod.

"Yes," I say. "The planet. We have been tasked with ushering her through this dark age and into a new and brighter future. Before the Devastation, Tajss was dying. The planet itself had been overworked, her riches stolen with such gleeful abandon that she wasn't going to survive."

"It sounds similar to what we were taught about our

home planet on the ship," she says. "That it had been left almost a wasteland from overpopulation and lack of environmental care."

"Quite similar, it would seem," I say. "The Devastation was the result of a Galactic War for the control of Tajss."

"I'd gathered as much," she says. "What does this have to do with us?"

Scratching my head, I try to work out the words.

"So many lives were lost," I say. "The Devastation was ages ago, and I loved before it, too. I've been thinking about that, a lot. If the dragon only chooses its soulmate, the other half of it, then where does the one who dies early go?"

"You mean the idea of heaven," she says.

"I don't know that word," I say.

"We believe that the souls move on to an eternal reward, a paradise," she says.

"Oh," I say. "That is not a concept that we Zmaj had. I'd never thought about it much. Mostly because of the bijass and the fog over my past, but now that I am remembering it's not something I thought about before either.

What I recall is that it was rare for mated pairs not to die close to each other, at the ends of their lives. If one did pass early, the other merely waited out their time. There was no second-chance love that I'd ever heard of anyway. There were not even stories of it."

"That sounds terrible and lonely," she says, frowning.

"Yes," I agree. "It was rare and usually only by accident that one was lost. But an eternal reward? What greater reward than there is to be with the one you love? Holding them in your arms, touching them, existing with them?"

"I always believed you were reunited with them after you die," she says.

"Then, what if…" I trail off, the thought too big for words.

"What if what?" she asks, scooting closer on her seat and leaning against me.

"What if the missing souls went to your planet?" I ask.

She sits up, staring, mouth opening then she closes it. Her concentration face appears, and a smile pulls at my lips recognizing it.

"It would mean..." she starts then trails off.

"Exactly," I say.

"How could we know?" she asks.

Rising to my feet, I sweep her into my arms and kiss her. A deep kiss, full of all the fiery passion that she arouses in me. Raging with the fire of the dragon, burning so hot it feels like my blood will boil out of my scales, too extreme to be contained in the flesh of my body. She wraps her legs around my waist, and I'm harder than I've ever been.

My cock throbs, pulsing with need for her. I run my hands over her perfect body, down to the curve of her ass.

Her exotically exposed breasts press against my chest. She moans as I groan, unable to contain the desire. It has to be expressed.

I carry her to the small bedroom of the quarters we have been quarantined into and close the door behind us with my tail.

She breaks the kiss and pulls her shirt over her head, throwing it to one side. Her bare breasts, boldly exposed unlike a female Zmaj, jut towards me inviting. The rosy tips are hard, straining, and I know from experience, oh so sensitive.

Gently I take one into my mouth, lightly brushing it with my tongue. She shudders and grinds her pussy against me. My cock pounds in response, pulling blood from all other parts of my body. My hearts beat faster to feed the prime cock's call.

She twines her hair in her hands tight, pulling me back

into her lips then kissing across my face. She nibbles on my ear.

"Fuck me," she whispers. "Give me that big fucking cock."

My cock was straining to break free, but now it is stiffer. Harder than ever before. Her words drive desire to new heights.

I set her on her feet, and she is working her pants off as I undo the tie of my own. I grab my erect member. Slowly, I stroke its hard length as she finishes pulling her pants off, sitting on the edge of the pallet.

She sees me stroking my cock and lies back onto her elbows, spreading her legs. Slowly, she trails her hand up her leg towards the soft mound of her womanhood.

Biting my lip, eyes closing to half, my vision is consumed by the movement of her fingers. She passes over her mound, the lips parting slightly to expose the wet pink folds but she keeps moving up.

Across her stomach towards her breasts. Goosebumps form in the trail of her fingers. My desire pounds as an orgasm builds to an inescapable edge. Her fingers circle the nipples of one breast, then the other.

"Anna," I groan.

A half smile forms on her face as she continues trailing the hand back down to her sex. I stroke myself slowly, watching the display of pure thrill. She flattens her hand across her mound, rubbing, and I know she is working her pleasure button.

She moans and her hips thrust towards me. It's all I can stand. My cock pulses, and the first of my come leaks watching her.

"You want me, come get it," she orders.

I am an obedient male. No hesitation. I kneel on the edge of the pallet and lean over her. My body covers her much smaller one as I hold myself over her with one arm, my other hand on my cock, moving it to her opening.

She touches my face. Trails of fire are left in the wake of her touch. She purses her lips, leans her head back, and moans as I press the head of my dick into her opening.

The wet warmth of her pussy grips me and a shiver races down my spine. My wings twitch in response. I move my tail up and use the tip to tease her nipples as I push deeper.

Her body opens itself to me, taking my cock until I'm fully seated inside of her. She gasps and moans as each ridge of my cock passes her opening and fills her. The sensation of her engulfing my member consumes all my thoughts.

She feels so good. The way we fit together, physically, mimics the way our spirts meld. Our bodies give reality to the spiritual.

She has her hands clasped around my neck and pulls herself up to meet my lips with a deep, passionate kiss. She drives her tongue into my mouth the same way and with the same rhythm as I drive my dick into her pussy.

Fully seated, I hold while our tongues continue their passion dance. She moves her hips in a slow circle, settling me more fully.

Time passes as we enjoy each other, slowly, taking our time and experiencing each moment fully. There is no rush—our time is ours to enjoy. We offer each other our bodies in full.

The dragon though, demands satisfaction. It wants to sow its seed, create a future for itself and its race.

I resist the primal instinct, holding deep, letting her guide the motion but the orgasm the dragon desires is building with every small motion she makes.

"Calaun," she moans, then pulls her hips down and back.

When only the tip of my dick remains inside her, she thrusts up, taking it fully in again, and I'm lost to the overwhelm of sensation. Primal instinct rules and together we thrust.

Hands move over each other. I use my tail to tease her breasts, too. We give each other pleasure as the demand for satisfaction builds in each of us. I'm rutting into her, claiming her with each thrust of my dick into her wet and accepting pussy.

Animal instinct is all. Drive in, pull out, drive in, reaffirming my mark. She is mine and I am hers. My treasure. My eternal desire.

I can't hold back, and from her moans and cries, I know she can't either.

One thrust, and it's almost there. I wrestle the orgasm into submission, waiting to be sure she is there with me.

"Yes!" she cries out and this is it.

I thrust back in, and this time I let it go. My seed explodes, filling her until it is spilling out past us. Her nails slide across the scales of my back as her body shudders and quakes with the force of her orgasm.

It goes and goes until at last it is spent. I lie down on her, kissing her neck, and she shudders pulling away.

"That tickles," she laughs, offering me her lips instead.

I take them. Mine.

"My treasure," I whisper.

"*My* treasure," she smiles.

16

ANNABEL

"It's been four days, and no one knows anything!" I grouch.

"It takes time," Calaun says, being unreasonably calm.

He's right, but that doesn't mean I like it. Four days of worry. The sex is great, and we're really clicking as a couple. I'm starting to believe his idea. It makes sense on some kind of deeply personal level. Resonating with a truth that I can't apply logic to.

"Time sucks," I say, throwing myself onto a chair.

Calaun sits down and takes my hand in his. He raises it to his lips, placing a sensual kiss. I smile and shake my head.

"How can I help?" he asks.

His calmness is an island in the storm of my emotions. I can't help but to look at the situation more logically because of him. His kindness, his understanding. He never argues or debates or tries to counter me when my emotions run away with me. It's always, how can he help. Nothing but pure understanding is all he ever gives me.

"It's nothing," I admit. "I'm going stir crazy."

"You are worried," he says, patting my hand.

"Yes," I admit. "I am."

"About me?" he asks.

Yes," I say. "What if you have whatever happened to Ladon? If it wasn't serious, we wouldn't still be in this quarantine. They're worried, and they're not telling us what's happening out there!"

He frowns and stares at the door. Someone comes several times a day. They bring food, water, check on us but no one who has come has had any answers. Ladon is not better is all we know, and none of them get close to us. They knock on the door, and we wait to answer until they've clearly had time to step back away.

My stomach knots up thinking about it. This is such an insane situation. Was there something in the air that escaped when he tried to break through that metal? Why did it affect him and not Calaun? Will it affect Calaun?

That's really it, isn't it? Will I lose him when I've only just found him?

My heart skips a beat, and my throat clenches tight as tears well in my eyes. He sees my distress and wraps his arms around, pulling me tight. His arms are my island. A place of safety I've not had in so long. In his arms I can let everything go, and I do.

I'm sobbing into his shoulder. I can't hold back. I don't know how long I weep against his chest, but at last I'm reduced to empty shuddering. He's taken all the fears away, and then there is only us.

He continues making soothing noises, hands running through my hair, down my back. Holding me until it's all gone. I'm drained. Even the fear is nothing but an empty husk.

"It will be fine," he says. "If I was going to be affected, it would have happened by now."

"You're right," I agree. "I'm sure, but I'm scared. We only

arrived at the City, Rosalind and I are getting along, but here I show up and this happens? It's terrible. What if… what if he…"

I can't say it out loud, but he tightens his grip.

"Ladon is very strong," he says. "He will be fine."

The door to our rooms pushes open causing me to jump. No one has been in the rooms with us since we were put into quarantine. It's not a regular person that walks in though, it's Malcolm.

"Hi." The small half-Zmaj boy waves as he walks in. He's so small and perfect but terror strikes deep into my heart seeing him.

"You can't be here!" I yell.

It doesn't affect him at all. He sighs and shakes his head.

"It's fine," he says. "My mom will be here soon. So will Addison."

"No," I say, fighting the urge to run and grab him up. "It's dangerous!"

If we're contagious we can't let him near us. I stand up and pull Calaun with me, backing away. Malcom rolls his eyes.

"You don't have it," he says, sitting down on the floor.

His tiny wings rustle and his tail swishes from side to side. He crosses his arms over his chest and stares at us.

"Malcolm, how do you know this?" I ask.

"Tajss says so," he says matter-of-factly.

"What did you say?" Calaun asks, sharp interest apparent in his voice.

"Why do big people always do that?" Malcolm asks.

"Do what?" I ask.

"Ask me to repeat what I say," he harrumphs. "It's not going to change. I said what I said because it's true. You can't change true. What's true is true!"

His anger and frustration does nothing but make him

look cuter still. It's ridiculous how adorable he is sitting there angrily glaring at us.

"And Tajss told you this?" Calaun asks.

"Yes," he says. "Who else would?"

"Do you speak to Tajss often?" Calaun asks.

I watch the exchange between the two of them with great interest. Calaun isn't treating Malcolm as a child at all, yet I'm filled with a certainty that he'd be an amazing father. Inside my belly, a warmth forms and I'm acutely aware of myself as a woman.

"Only when she wants to," Malcolm shrugs.

"Do you have any food? I'm hungry," he says.

Footsteps sound outside the door, and then its thrown wide. Amara bursts into the room in a fury.

"Malcolm!" she exclaims scooping him up into her arms. "You cannot do that!"

"I'm sorry, Mommy," he says, holding his tiny arms out to her. She pulls him close, and he hugs her, kissing her check. "I got bored, and you were coming here next."

"I didn't say that!" Amara says as Addison appears in the door looking haggard and out of breath too.

"I'm in no shape for this," Addison pants, leaning on the door frame.

"Distancing!" I burst out.

"You're… fine…" Addison huffs.

I tighten my grip on Calaun's arm and try not to shake. "You're sure?"

"Yes," Addison says.

"I told you," Malcolm says. "No need to be the big hero… yet."

Fresh tears form in the corners of my eyes, but now they're tears of relief.

"Is Ladon better?" Calaun asks.

Amara and Addison share a look that says very clearly

that he is not. I swallow hard to push down the bile rising in my throat.

"He is in a coma," Addison says.

"How do you know we are not contagious?" Calaun asks.

"It's been four days," Addison says. "You've had no symptoms. The others have shown symptoms in that time."

"Others?" I ask, dread making my voice shake.

"Sverre and Ormarr have both fallen sick," Addison says.

"Ormarr?" Calaun asks. "It reached the Tribe?"

"Unfortunately, yes," Addison says. "Ormarr came to help with Ladon. He developed a fever as well."

Calaun looks at me. His frown is deep and thoughtful.

"I need to report to the Order," he says.

"Oh," I say, my stomach hitting the floor.

"They must be told about this. Maybe our healers know something that will help," he says.

"Of course," I agree, but I'm sick to my stomach.

"Treasure?" he asks, dipping down to meet my downcast eyes. "What is it?"

I shake my head, struggling to hold back unshed tears.

"Please, tell me," he says.

He grips my arms, anchoring me to him, drawing out the words I don't want to say.

"I can't," I say, shaking my head.

"Of course you can," he says. "You are amazing and can do anything."

I laugh despite myself. A short, harsh bark of a laugh, but a laugh, nonetheless. He places a gentle hand under my chin and lifts my head until our eyes meet. He sparkles through the unshed tears. He wipes one away as it falls down my cheek.

"It's selfish," I admit.

"Nothing about you is selfish," he reassures me. "You give

all you are and have for those you care about. It's one of the many things I love about you."

"I don't want you to go," I blurt out. "I don't want to be without you."

It's an admission of everything I've felt to a degree I'm not comfortable with. I've never wanted to depend on anyone. Even before the crash I was independent, and in that was my strength. My ability to carry on, no matter what. This feeling of emptiness, and almost fear at the idea of him not being by my side is terrifying.

"Then come with me," he says.

"Come with you?" I ask, feeling my eyes widen as the surprise of it takes me. "But… I can't. The Order is… secretive. They won't want me there. I'd be outcast, or you would be, and I don't want to do that to you."

"My sweetest treasure," he says. "You see? Even now you consider yourself selfish when what you're truly concerned with is me. How is that selfish?"

Swallowing hard, I force the lump out of my throat.

"Are you serious?" I ask, sticking to the point.

"Yes," he says. "Very much so."

"But… won't they object?" I ask.

"I do not believe so, no," he says. "They might not let you into the inner workings, but I do not see any problem with you visiting with me. We'll be separated while I report but, my truest love, I cannot stand the idea of being without you."

"Me either!" I cry and throw my arms around him.

Amara clears her throat loudly.

"Uhm, not to interrupt an emotional moment, but there are little ones present," she says.

"Oh!" I exclaim having completely forgotten about Malcolm.

He's watching us with great interest.

"You love?" he asks, pointing at Calaun.

"Yes," I answer. "Yes, I do."

Malcolm nods thoughtfully. "You love?"

He points to me addressing his question to Calaun.

"With all I am," Calaun says.

Malcolm nods and frowns, staring off into the distance. It's as if he's looking at someone else or talking in his head with someone none of us can see. At last he smiles, and his eyes focus on the here and now.

"This is good," Malcolm says. "You've found each other."

It feels like something hit me in the stomach, and a cold chill races down my limbs.

"What do you mean by that, Malcolm?" I ask.

He's plopped down and playing with a stick on the floor. He looks up when I ask my question, but something about his face is different. He doesn't have the aura he did of someone older than his years. He looks, for all the world, like a toddler playing on the floor. A strange, alien toddler with scales, wings, and a tail, but a toddler none the less.

"What?" he asks.

"Don't bother," Amara says. "The moment is gone, he won't remember any of it now."

"What moment? What was that?" I ask.

Amara and Addison exchange a look then they both shrug.

"We don't know," Addison admits.

The look on her face makes it seem painful that she has to admit as much.

"What are you doing about Ladon and Ormarr then?" I ask.

"Everything we can," Addison says. "I'm not a xeno-biologist. I've learned a lot but I'm no expert on Zmaj physiology. Still, we're doing all we can. First and foremost is a lockdown. No more traveling between the City, Mining Settlement, or the Tribe Cave.

Everyone in the City is on lockdown, and I've asked everyone to keep distance from each other. It's all we can do right now to try and spread the slow of it."

"But you two are here together?" I ask.

"So far it's only affected Zmaj," Addison says. "I suspect humans are immune to it, but we might be carriers. I'm running tests on that now."

"And you're obviously not sick," Amara says to Calaun.

"I'll ask the Order for help," Calaun offers.

"Good, we need it," Addison says. "Ladon seems fine, physically, but he won't wake up. Here is a copy of all my notes on what I've observed. Can you take them to your doctors for me?"

"Of course," Calaun says.

"Good," Addison says. "I've already spoken to Rosalind, and she knows you'll most likely be going with him. You two should leave as fast as possible. Avoid contact with anyone else in the City, and I'd recommend you keep at least a six-foot space between you and any member of the Order."

"Six feet?" Calaun asks.

"If the illness is airborne, as I suspect, then hopefully that will be enough to keep it from jumping to anyone you come in contact with," Addison says.

"I understand," Calaun says.

The two women gather up Malcolm and take their leave. My heart is beating erratically, and my chest is tight. I can't quit thinking that something might happen to Calaun. He notices my listlessness and takes me in his arms.

"I'm scared," I whisper.

"I know," he says. "But listen, Tajss did not bring us together across all these impossibilities of time and space to tear us apart. She is not cruel like that."

"But what if?" I ask, unable to fill in the *if* part of the question because there are too many things that could go there.

"What if?" he asks, shrugging. He peppers my face with kisses, holding me tight. "'What if' is the path to darkness. We must be in the moment. Live for the now, and we'll create our future by what we do right this moment."

"I can't lose you," I say.

"You won't," he says, kissing me again. "I am yours. You are mine. We always have been, we always will be."

"Millions of light-years can't separate us," I smile.

"The entire galaxy can't keep us apart," he says.

"Nothing in the universe?" I ask.

"Nothing," he answers, then drives his tongue into my mouth.

Desire flashes hot and burns away the worries and concerns.

"How…" I pant, breaking the kiss. "How long do we have?"

"Enough time," he says, his voice heavy with lust. "There is always enough time, for you."

He grabs my waist and tosses me into the air, catching me and settling me on his hips. I wrap my legs around his waist, and we kiss deeper.

"If you're sure…"

"I am," he says, his hard cock digging into my pussy, carrying me towards our pallet.

I struggle out of my shirt as we move, throwing it to one side. As I wrap my arms around him, and my breasts are crushed between us, certainty comes over me.

This may be a trying time, but every moment since the crash of the ship has been. I know, now, that everything will be better. No matter what happens, if it's hard or easy it doesn't matter because the two of us will be together.

Together with an alien man who is the other half of me. My treasure. My soulmate.

"I love you," I gasp as he thrusts his cock in.

"I love you, my treasure," he says and our bodies' joining is symbolic of the joining of our souls. "Forever."

"Forever," I agree.

The End

ABOUT THE AUTHOR

USA Today Bestselling Author of fantasy and scifi romance, Miranda Martin's books feature larger than life heroes with out-of-this-world anatomy and smart heroines destined to save the world. As a little girl she would sneak off with her nose in a book, dreaming of magical realms. Today she brings those fantasies to life and adores every fan who chooses to live in them for a while.

She was born and raised in southern Virginia, but as a veteran she's traveled to places like Korea, Hawaii and good 'ole Texas. Now she's settled in Kansas, the heart of America, with her husband and daughters. Her favorite animals are dragons, unicorns and cats. If she's not writing, you can still find her tucked away somewhere with a warm blanket and her nose in a book.

Get in touch!

mirandamartinromance.com

miranda@mirandamartinromance.com

Made in the USA
Middletown, DE
09 February 2025

71044487R00106